The Museum was not very popular . . .

After all, who wanted to see what life had been like in the old days? When people got bent and stiff with age (ghastly) and kids had diseases. (That's what they called it when you were *ill*.)

Of course you knew the living, moving re-creation of scenes from ancient life weren't real people —only androids—but still, they were so realistic it was sort of morbid. Aside from teaching history, it was a puzzle why Central Control kept the Museum going really.

Still, it made you realize how lucky you were, not to have been alive when people went on and on until they died naturally . . .

THE
RESURRECTION
OF
ROGER DIMENT

Douglas R. Mason

BALLANTINE BOOKS • NEW YORK
An Intext Publisher

BALLANTINE BOOKS, INC.
101 Fifth Avenue, New York, N. Y. 10003

CONTENTS

CHAPTER ONE

Roger Diment felt a band of pressure round his eyes and reckoned hazily that his chaplet must have slipped.

He tried to push it back on his broad forehead and found that his hands moved together for a few centimeters and then stopped. They were taped that way. Also his legs at knee and ankle.

Sensors beating back to full strength sent in a whole sheaf of data that threatened to turn his mind in stumbling retreat to the limbo it had just now left.

But Diment had not been a top athlete for nothing. He forced himself to a deep-breathing session and worked doggedly at the clues he had. For a start, he was lying on his left side with his knees drawn up almost to his chest, naked as any needle and all set for urn burial.

Secondly, he was cold. He was lying on a smooth metal tray that was doing a good job of spreading his thermal agitation to all parts, and that inexorable Second Law was against his gathering any of it back.

Thirdly, there was a movement of air across his cold skin, and even as he registered it as a fact, he knew that he was the moving object. There was enough to give a confident sitrep. He was hogtied on a conveyor. Now he knew what it was all about and was almost stunned by despair.

He had known it would come in his thirtieth year. Everyone had that much foreknowledge. But he did not know when. He was one of the early ones, in the first monthly batch, then. That was the unexpected thing.

Probably right to the end of the year, the Wayfarer age group did not believe it would happen to them in spite of annual clearance. Next year's Wayfarers would be the same. God, this time last year he had not given it a thought.

Still, this was a poor way to go. Did it always happen or was he unfortunate or just drug-resistant?

Unfortunate? What kind of word was that? It was unfortunate to be dead or unconscious. To be conscious even of discomfort was pure gain. Using all his strength and nearly dislocating his neck, he got his hands to the bandage and managed to pull it down.

It stabilized over his mouth, but he could not make the effort again. Anyway there was nothing to say. At least he could see that he was not alone.

The conveyor was moving very slowly through a dimly lit conduit with a gentle downward slope. Straining up against his thongs, he could look up the line to a succession of pale mounds following him on his journey, still as plastic lay figures. Nobody else was making a thing about it.

How had it been done? For a short count curiosity, evolution's handmaid, diverted his mind from the present to what had happened.

It had been the first of the continuous round of parties which the Wayfarer age group held throughout their last year. Staged in the biggest pleasure dome on the offshore island of Xanadu, it had played a tattoo on every exquisite square of sense. Any more unconfined and Joy would have split down the middle.

Diment remembered arriving at the quay in his cabin cruiser, perfumes blowing about and the isle full of noises.

The conveyor gave a small jolt and a ripple went away in the distance, sheep over an imaginary stile. Of course they would bring the bodies back for disposal. There would be a tunnel to connect with the converter. He was shortly due to donate his eighty kilograms of well-coordinated flesh to the public use, organ bank, blood pool, a handful of useful chemicals, soap even. He might finish his earthly run as a lather in some girl's bubble bath.

Facing it squarely, he reckoned he was worth more than that. He jack-knifed round until he could get purchase with his feet against the thick beading which edged the conveyor belt. Then he began to straighten out until he felt that he would rupture every muscular wall in his body sack.

Something had to go. It was the loop that bound his hands to a shackle on the deck. The resultant of all the forces shot him at an angle off the disassembly line like any flying Gandharvas.

He hit the curved wall of the conduit and rebounded into the well with only enough sense left in his head to roll convulsively out of the caterpillar track.

Diment lay still, weighing the angles. In spite of the subterranean chill on his bare skin, he was slippery with sweat. Dangerous living might well increase sensitivity, but he had been near enough minced to doubt it.

His hands were still clamped together, but he could move them to his face and clear the band from his mouth. Then he found the end of the sticky tape with his teeth and began to pull it off.

How long it took he could never tell, but the tumbril rolled slowly on. So many, he would not have thought the bell had tolled for so many.

Part of his mind ran a calculation on times and distances. Somewhere at the delivery end, he was going to be missed. The man-made island was a good two kilometers off-shore. Supposing he had gotten halfway before he woke up. That meant a kilometer to go. Over half an hour at the pace of the conveyor.

Which way should he go? The island was very small and difficult to leave without being seen. The mainland was the better bet. Also another thought struck him. Arrivals would be checked off. If he could shift a few along the line, they would be looking for somebody else.

Stooping in the narrow space, Diment worked up a jog trot that doubled the speed of the conveyer. For as far ahead as he could see, there was no gap in the moving line. He was beginning to think that he had never been part of it. Then a small incline helped him to spot his empty nest as it flattened to take the new level.

As he paced it, he could read off a large number designed for computer scanning: 216.

He forged ahead and began to work on 215. It was very tricky, half bent over and still running; but he got the shackle free and straightened up for a breather.

It was a man who could be already dead. Respiration was so slow he could not detect it. Moving him against the ongoing thrust of the conveyer was easy, and he retied the rope.

Up the line once more, he found that 214 was female, a lush, pink Renoir. That would be better. They would be looking for a woman.

By the time he had shifted her to 215's vacant slot, there was another change in level. The conveyer was moving up on the home run.

Diment crouched beside the moving track, breathing hard. The empty station disappeared up ahead, and he was no nearer finding a program. Now that the immediate call for action was done, the lingering effects of the general anesthetic had to be reckoned with. Also the regular flow of bodies had a hypnotic effect. He was being presented with a majority vote. He was a minority of one with no rights under the system.

His abstracted gaze came to focus on a smoothly contoured can, which had a familiar look even among so many. Recognition was helped by three small moles in a neat equilateral triangle which had been a familiar feature. A long black ringlet coiled on the platform like a lustrous rope clinched the deal. It was Pamela Harte, no other, bound for disposal like so much trash.

He paced the conveyer trying to work it out. How could he know whether resurrection and its pitfalls would be welcome? It might anyway be short-lived and the exercise would have to be done over with foreknowledge of what was to come.

He examined his own case. Naked, cold, and with a very tricky future, he was glad to be alive. She could at least have the chance to decide.

There was not much time. A hundred meters ahead, the conveyer disappeared through a hanging flap of flexible metal cloth like a one-way valve.

Twenty meters off, he had her free and propped her against the wall while he peeled away the strappings at wrist and ankle and pulled the band from her eyes.

It was a surprise to find that they were wide open, almost all pupil surrounded by a narrow ring of flecked hazel. But when he passed his hand across, there was not even a flicker to show interest.

Her left hand was tightly clenched, and he pried back the fingers one at a time. In the palm was a single diamond earclip. She had made a bid to beat the old maxim that there were no pockets in a shroud. That argued at least a determined toehold on the land of the living. Maybe she would welcome a reprieve at that.

Until this last Wayfarer Year, a busy time as a small arms specialist had not left much slack for boning up on the medicare of stoned birds. But he did his best, working her arms up and down and lightly slapping her cheeks in a routine dimly remembered from an actualizer serial, where the female protagonist had to be brought round every other reel after one crisis or another.

It was one more illustration, if one were needed, that truth had it over fiction every time. Pamela Harte's circumstances were as bizarre as they could get.

The action was at least doing good to the Samaritan. Diment felt warmer than at any time yet in the sequence and only needed a couple of words from his punchbag to make him feel all agog.

When he got them, he reckoned he had not known when he was well off. Pamela Harte snapped into the present on a rising note of delight saying, "Roger, you cunning improviser. Where have you taken me?" and wound her arms round his neck in a carryover from action suspended when the sedative had struck home.

Belatedly, Diment realized he had made a bad choice out of the hundreds passing by. When you had said she was good at what she was good at, you had said all. Being a discreet fugitive was not on the manifest. Any time at all, some monitoring gear was going to signal that it had found an empty stall. She would have to be convinced but quick.

He unwound her arms and pushed her back with one hand flat on her mobile chest until she was pinned to the wall. Then he used the other to knock her head rhythmically against the dado to punctuate his urgent communiqué, "Hear this and let it sink right in, Pamela. You know the score. You're a Wayfarer. It's come sooner than we thought. Now we see it from inside. Something nobody mentions when friends don't appear for breakfast. I was on this disposal chute, but the drug wore off and I got clear. Then you came along and, God help me, I took you off of the line. The question is, do you want to stay off or would you sooner take it now, since you're halfway there. I can knock you cold and dump you back on the tumbril if that's the way you want it."

There was no doubt that the message was going home. After its period of rest, her data acquisition network was clearly pulling out all the stops. Always expressive, her eyes mirrored surprise, fear, bewilderment, and something enigmatic which defied the researcher.

It could have been mere pique, because she said, "You can stop doing that, you big ape. I'm not stupid. Let me think."

"Well make it quick. Time is not on our side."

Thinking had not been her preferred activity;

but it was a limited choice question. In five seconds she had her answer pat. "You can unclench that ham-like fist. What have I to lose? I'll go along with you."

Diment had picked up her earclip and held it out on his palm. "A rebirthday gift. You were clutching it in your hot little hand when I pulled you off the ghost train."

"It's not much of a birthright."

"Don't grumble. Naked we leave this world and naked we return to it."

"That's a point. We're conspicuous like this. It's a very dressy age in the public sector."

Diment was conscious that there had been a change in their limited scene. The conveyer, still moving slowly at his back, was making more noise. It was off load. The last subject was six places up the line. Empty trays numbered 1006, 1007, 1008 were sliding by.

He said curtly, "Let's go, then," and led off with Eurydice three places to the rear, grumbling about her feet.

By shortening the life span, society had made it all go for its children. With the menarche stabilized at age ten for male and female and education refined and streamlined to a minimum time scale, they were out and about for their brief, full-power blaze at an early age. There was no time to stand and stare. Consequently, Diment had not familiarized himself with the disposal end of the cycle. What lay ahead was unknown.

Thinking on his feet, he reckoned that there would be no human operator at this level. He had never heard of anybody being in the mortician business.

It would be handled by androids or a fully auto-mated system. On the other hand, there would be a fair bristle of scanning devices on and around the conveyer. They would have to legislate for the odd case opting for out.

At the metal cloth curtain, he stopped dead, and Pamela Harte, still preoccupied about her feet, blundered pneumatically into his back, grabbing him by reflex to save balance.

He said unjustly, "Save it, Pamela. There isn't time," and lifted a corner of the screen.

The conveyor ran on for five meters in a widening tunnel, which finally opened into a large, oblong operations area.

Warm air funneling back explained the need for a barrier. Too much heat along the way might perk up the clientele.

At the far end, crossing at right angles and moving from left to right, a series of supplementary conveyers passed over the line and disappeared into square ports spaced out along the right hand wall.

It was from these that the heat came together with a pink glow whenever a hatch opened.

They were in time to see the last half dozen of the nine hundred and ninety-eight make the journey. Androids spaced along the production line had the chore broken down into simple units.

Blood was drawn off into overhead extraction circuits. Main areas of fatty tissue were flensed away by a purpose-built group with vibrator extensions on both wrists and loaded cleanly into stainless steel tubs that ran alongside the conveyer and then wheeled away through a side door. Some selected organs designated for preservation as transplants were hived off by the next busy group. The residue went to the incinerators.

It was practical. It was efficient. Nobody was complaining. But Pamela, who had been overcome by curiosity and had shoved her head under Diment's arm, had seen enough. Her stomach was making a serious bid to turn itself inside out.

The last lingering effects of the sedative died the death for Diment. He was stone cold sober and felt that he had doubled his age. Knowing intellectually that some such process was likely was one thing. Seeing it in the flesh was another. He dropped the curtain and knelt down beside the girl.

Very gently he put an arm around her shaking shoulders and pulled her round toward him. Warm tears fell on his chest as he stroked her hair and said anything that came into his head. There was no conscious element of sex in it. Human solidarity in the face of a problem which was basically insoluble. Words that finally penetrated, so that she was listening and the deep trembling grew less.

He knew he was winning when she started to argue, "But not like *that*. It shouldn't be like *that*. Why do we allow that?"

"How long has the Federation been set up?"

"I don't know. Centuries. Longer. I'm not a Researcher."

"So long that we don't think about it. This is the pattern all over the Western Hemisphere, and the East is mainly wasteland. It's tried and tested and it works. Except for an accident, we wouldn't know or care."

Female logic had a ready answer to that one. "But now we do know, so we have to care."

"We have a good life. You enjoyed yourself, didn't you? We accept that we don't have to face illness or growing old."

"Those are words. We don't know whether that was bad or not. Anyway you should talk. You got me here. What do we do now?"

"That's a very good question. The short answer

is we get out of here and take a look outside. You don't look like a Wayfarer. You could be finishing your second decade. If we can get away from Barnston City we have a chance."

"But we shall grow old and then they will know."

"It doesn't happen overnight. We'll cross that bridge when we come to it."

Long-term issues partially settled, her mind found snags closer at hand. "Which way do we go? I can't go through there."

"Why not? It's all over for now."

"You understand they were alive when they got there?"

"I've been thinking about that. It would be just as easy to put a killer in the knockout drop. But that wouldn't do. They want the transplant organs in top working order as they go to deep freeze. What you don't feel you don't know about. It's as broad as it's long. Those transplants ensure that up to Wayfarer age, we have a hundred per cent replacement service for accidental damage. It's logical."

"There aren't as many accidents as all that. I don't know of one by name."

She was keeping the conversation going, but it was a point and Diment had no answer. Maybe there had been a time when it was necessary and nobody had revised the system to keep it up to date. Come to think, nobody he had ever met knew what the system was. They were all too busy filling their thirty-year span with distance run.

He left it hanging about and took another look into the terminal. There was a waft of formaldehyde. The labor force was sluicing down the working area and each other with high power jets of white foamy liquid. It was almost playful.

Reluctant fascination had drawn Pamela to try again. She said bitterly, "You see. They don't care. It's all comedy to them. Anytime at all one of them could start in throwing a custard pie."

Hoses cut after a measured period and were dropped back into clips on the staging. Extractor fans started up and drew off the damp air. The conveyer stopped.

The androids balanced themselves, feet astride, and, starting from the far end, their operation lights winked out. Roof ports which had given brilliant light dropped to a glimmer. A long computer, spread halfway up the left-hand wall and served by a catwalk with a handrail, stopped its flickering pattern of tell-tales and settled for a moody amber glow.

Diment reckoned it was as well they hadn't moved before. Somewhere else there was a monitor. Some overlord system had followed the action and had switched off when there was no more to do. Following from that, there would have been a note made that two stations were empty. A fall-back organization would be checking along to find out why. Even now, very now, they could have started along the tunnel from the far end.

He grabbed the girl's wrist and shoved the curtain aside. Then he went through, keeping close to the wall.

As she came out hanging back at full arm's stretch, roof ports in the tunnel at her back stepped up their light level. The search was on.

Ushered anew into the world by her own startled "Eek," she closed up on the leader in a quick twist.

Nothing moved. The androids had done their stint and were resting their cogs. It could have been any automated packing bay between shifts.

Diment was thinking it out. He felt that he had aged a lifetime over the last half hour. For one thing, he had responsibilities. Having pulled the Harte off of the line, he owed her some kind of future. It was an unfamiliar situation. Over the normal thirty-year span, Mother State's everlasting arms supported her members. Even children were the special care of professionals who chose the work. Eugenically engineered from the outset, a citizen only had himself on his mind. Complete selfishness had become a national duty and way of life.

Work was said to be a therapy. A simple task might get her moving. He said, "Look around, Pamela. There must be a way into this place. Every once in a while, a human operator will have to check that the gear is in adjustment."

A way in would be a way out. It was the first good idea she had heard in a long time. She even moved two paces away from the wall to get a better look at it.

Except for the incinerator ports, the right-hand wall was solid. Far down the line, the end wall appeared to cross from edge to edge without break. The conveyer disappeared into the floor before it followed the full length of the hall.

It had to be the side they were on, but the computer spread filled most of it. They went along in single file over a ridged tile floor that was rough on the feet, climbed half a dozen open metal steps, and passed the presiding genius of the place.

Diment felt a rail turn under his hand and stopped. Twisting and pressing with a bare foot against a stanchion, he worked out a meter length. Holding it like a club, he swung it about to get the balance. Like the First Man with a broken

branch, he felt it was some counterweight to naked-
ness.

The squaw stood by. Having no button to twist,
she nervously smoothed her ringlet, which was hanging forward to her sternum. She was regretting the
current style. It was too handy. Any time at all she
might be dragged along by it.

Speech, however, was still on a sophisticated level.
Homo habilis said mildly, "How are you feeling
now? Ready to leap about in the sun?"

"I'll feel better when we get out of this place. But
I don't see what we can do. Where will we go? How
will we live?"

"Questions, questions. I should have known three
moles were no basis for choice, wherever sited."

"What's that supposed to mean?"

"Scrub round it. Let's get on or we'll still end up
dissected. Sorry."

He had to steady her as she swayed under a brief
return of vertigo. Then she was struggling away,
hazel eyes fairly glinting with sudden anger.

"You just don't care. You're an insensitive clod.
I'd be better off if you'd left me alone."

She broke free and ran ahead along the catwalk,
a living proof, if any were needed, that beauty lies
with the curve in action.

It was a small pleasure to watch, and Diment
appreciated it. 914–610–914 at a guess. About 1.6
meters tall. Compact and proportionate. Hardly due
for disposal. What was society thinking about? When
she dived off left, seemingly into the bowels of the
computer, the functional hall seemed suddenly very
lonely and rank with death.

He pushed up his pace and called once, "Pamela,"
all ready to apologize in the cause of good relations.
There was no answer. Level with the spot where she

had done her jack rabbit trick, he looked down a meter-wide gap between two consoles and said again, "Pamela. Don't mess about. Where are you?"

The alcove ran two meters back to a ridged bulkhead. Sides were solid. There was no place to go.

He prodded the floor and moved his weight slowly on to it, ready to grab either side if it sank away.

He was balanced on the balls of his feet, ready to move, when the corrugated wall slid smartly aside and an android standing four square in the opening lifted a hand with a power syringe in the pointing index finger.

Flattened sideways, Diment felt the compressed air riffle through the hair on his chest. He had a flash picture of a white-tiled corridor leading up at an angle with a second android already some paces off carrying the girl head down over its shoulder.

Anger flared redly through his brain. It was, above all, an insult. A diabolical liberty. They were being treated like vermin to be exterminated by remote control. Feedback had told the android that the shot had traveled farther than the target, and it was tracking round to a new aim when Diment shoved off from his backrest in a total mobilization of all available horsepower.

The rod flailed down and beat the moving arm, cracking off the plug-in hand unit at the wrist. Momentum carried Diment on. There was no room to swing his club again. His chest hit the smooth carapace of the android. He dropped the rod and grabbed for the bland oval head with both hands.

Programmed to seek out a designated quarry and shoot in a tranquilizing charge, the android was slow to adjust to the violent life. Before relays had dropped to authorize defensive action, the day was lost. Diment had bent its flexible neck to a point of no return, at right angles to the torso. Still standing upright, its visual sensors could only take data from the ceiling.

It stumbled slowly past, into the catwalk, where it hit the rail and pivoted forward into the hall.

Diment picked up his club and padded after the abductor. That one kept to its brief and carried on without a backward look. Either it thought that its partner was well able to look after itself or it couldn't care less. Pamela Harte's ringlet, hanging straight down, brushed its gunmetal thighs.

Diment chose his spot and swung two-handed for the center of its dome. In cold blood he would have been hung up thinking about the damage to the two-time loser if he missed. But the adrenalin boost nipping smartly round his synapses had short-circuited caution.

The casque dented in a three-centimeter groove, pop rivets scattered like buck shot, and the android stopped dead with its left leg raised for the next stop. A gyro stabilizer in its right calf kept it upright, but it was out of program.

Diment lifted the girl clear and propped her against the tiles to take stock. There was a small pink puncture mark over the ogee arch of her left breast. She was well out. No amount of slap and tickle was going to make any difference. She needed a quiet nook to sleep it off.

Companionship was coming at a high price. Maybe he should take her at her word. She was back now where she had been, in her private castle of unknowing, before he broke through the thicket.

But he was brought up short by the terrible vulnerability of the sleeping face. Calm and composed. Long dark lashes evenly spread. Nobody had a right to make that choice for anybody. At the same time, a stubborn streak made its statement. He had been pushed far enough. He was getting out and she was going with him until she could choose to use her vote.

He picked her up and draped her over his shoulder. For all practical purposes she was no better off. Identical means but different ends. The upward slope was just enough to make it very heavy going. He stopped thinking and set his teeth.

A hundred meters on, there was a choice. The tunnel split three ways. Since those using the system would know where they were going, there was no route post to help out.

Diment leaned his comely cross on a buttress and tried to figure where he would be in relation to the ground above. The conveyer had crossed to the mainland; that was sure. Tunnels being expensive, it was likely that it had taken the shortest line. That would mean somwehere left of the Marina. He tried to visualize the waterfront. What was next to the pool along the foreshore? A long tall block with twin towers. But of course, the medicenter. Medicare records and specialist consultant rooms for the Region. Transplant storage would be under that lot.

Beyond the medicenter was a long plateau with statuary and fountains and the Library and Museum complex. Not overused these days. Quietly rotting away. There had been talk of flattening the precinct and putting in a new stadium.

It was enough to give a direction. He would bear right at every intersection and try to surface in that area.

Pamela Harte had nothing to say. But he could feel her diaphragm moving. It was company of a kind. He pressed on at a steady walk, still climbing.

Time meant nothing. Place was a succession of white-tiled walls and dim amber roof ports spaced twenty paces apart. For his money, he was due to break out at any point from Land's End to The Wash.

When the lights flared into brilliance and a distant siren began a rhythmic pulsing wail, he went on three steps, thinking that it was all happening in his head.

But when he stood still, the noise was still there. A supplementary gurgle from the abdomen at his left ear confirmed that all the signals were external to himself and had the hallmark of truth.

It was likely enough. A party moving down the conveyer tunnel would have found the androids. Knowing it could not be mice, they had called a posse.

CHAPTER TWO

Iron-tongued clamor was coming from all sides. Diment had an insight into the use of noise as a weapon. It numbed his brain. In the open, he would not have known which way to run. As it was, choice was limited to up or down, and it seemed likely that the van would be round the last bend any time at all.

He pushed up his pace to a heroic jog trot, slippery with sweat, so that his Waltzing Mathilda was difficult to hold over his shoulder. Fifty meters ahead, the corridor veered left. It was a mark to aim for.

Ten meters from the corner, he had to slow to hitch Pamela back to her point of balance. A new rhythmic clank added itself to the orchestration.

Bitterly, he watched three androids in line abreast forge round the distant bend below.

They were jet black, squarer in the cowl than any he had seen; squat, even allowing for the vagaries of perspective. A piece of tubular rail was no armament at all against them. At the pace they were going, they would be tapping him on the shoulder in three minutes flat. He could say, "They went thataway"—but it would not be believed.

A hornet whine stung him on. Some small, fast-moving projectile whammed past and ricocheted at the facing wall. He was not going to be saved for his working parts. The word had gone out to take him dead.

Diment reached the turn with his lungs laboring under strain. Ahead, there was another hundred meters of empty corridor. He dashed the sweat out of his eyes and looked at it. There was not a hope in hell of reaching the far end.

Firing had stopped. With the quarry out of sight there was no motivation. Feet pounding in unison were coming near.

Like an earlier model in a cave mouth, he put the girl behind him and stood feet astride, lips writhed away to show his eyeteeth, short hairs in a bristle. An amalgam of fear, anger, and over-riding hate for the androids who were running him down built up complete disregard for himself as a person. It was as good as an anesthetic. He was all set for a suicidal sortie as soon as the first flick of black metal came into vision.

Consequently, he was badly prepared for infiltration from the rear. Hands clamped on him before he could swing his club. He was dragged backward, feet half off the deck, with a sickly sweet pad clamped over his nose and mouth.

Last thoughts were that he had been cheated again. Nobody was going to let him meet it in his own way. It was an invasion of privacy that could not be justified on any count. Then resistance sagged. Overwhelming pity for Pamela Harte and all the Wayfarers, of all times, filled his mind. He heard a voice shouting, "You can't do it," before the scene blacked.

Diment was struggling. Thrashing about trying to get a grip on whoever was holding him down. Somebody was saying in a deep, rumbling basso profundo, "Easy. Easy now. Take it easy. You're all right."

The hand on his chest was lightweight, soothing if anything. He heaved himself up and opened his eyes.

He was sitting on a low, upholstered divan, and the hand which transferred intelligently to support his back was Pamela Harte's. She was left of his narrow cot, zipped modestly into white coveralls, but easily identifiable by her ringlet, which was tickling his neck.

On the right, the speaker said, "Easy" again. This one was a total stranger and rough on a subject waking from drugged sleep.

Diment had never seen anything like him off the miniature screen of a teaching video and was not reassured. He was hauling himself off the couch ready to sell his blood dear, when Pamela, sensing his mood, said urgently, "Hold it, you big ape. He's on your side. At least I think so."

Movement had sent Diment's head in a slow spin and he dropped back into bed. If it was true, it was just as well. He couldn't fight his way out of a paper bag. The room stabilized and he looked again.

The man was massively built and wore clothes of antique cut. Baggy pants that finished below the knee, long gray stockings, heavy brown shoes. He had a brown jacket, a check shirt buttoned to the neck, and a strip of narrow cloth knotted at the collar that hung freely down the convex slope of a barrel chest. His face extended without barrier into the top of his head, hair being concentrated into two bushy outcrops over the ears.

A ham-like hand shot out and Diment believed for a split second that Pamela had got it all wrong and the true hostile act was about to begin. But the protuberant blue eyes were mild enough and the voice was rumbling. "Bedall. Harry Bedall. Sorry about the Mickey. Couldn't take any chances. It was a close run thing. Glad to meet you. No ill feelings, I hope."

Diment took the proferred hand which was warm and hard and recognizably human. He copied the manners of the country. "Diment. Roger Diment."

"So I believe. So this young girl with you said."

That was an odd way of looking at it. As Wayfarers, they were both as old as anybody could get. But then Bedall was something else. He could be ninety. All judgment was comparative in the end.

Recall flooded in and Diment recognized he owed a debt to somebody. He said, "As I remember, we were just about through. I guess we owe you our thanks."

"Think nothing of it, son. But I won't say it hasn't raised a few problems. You did a lot yourself. If you hadn't got so far, we'd have left you to work it out for yourselves. It wasn't popular with everybody, I can tell you."

"Where are we, then?"

"Well as to that, you'll have to wait until we see whether you can be fitted in. It wouldn't be sensible to tell you too much until we know more about you. You could be a plant."

"A plant?"

"Two plants if you like. A gorgeous little plant and a big ugly plant. We've been operating a long

time, and even the high speed idiots that run the
region must have noticed something. I wouldn't put
it past them to ship an agent along the conveyer
in the hope that he might stumble on to a lead."

It was all gobbledegook to Diment. He said, however, "That would have to be a dedicated man. If
he found no evidence, he'd end up disemboweled.
Or haven't you seen the payoff?"

"I've seen it and it makes me sick to my stomach.
How do you feel now? If you can make it, we'll
get a little farther on. There's bound to be a big
search, and they have some very refined detector
gear for picking up human brain currents."

Diment swung his legs off the bed and stood up.
Now he could see clearly, but there was no dramatic
jump in credibility. Nothing had prepared him to
be wakened in a greenroom. There were other people about, all dressed as if for a costume ball. The
room was large, square, low-ceilinged. Basket containers were littered about. Round the walls or pulled
out into the room were long racks on swivel castors.
He was suddenly conscious that he was the only
nude on the set.

Bedall seemed to appreciate his dilemma and
gave a cheerful bark of laughter. "It'll disappoint
the women, but we'd better find you something to
wear." He fished about on a free-standing rack
with sets of clothing hanging in plastic dust covers.
"Try this."

It was a full outfit. Briefs. Heavily striped shirt,
narrow cord trousers, red socks, soft leather shoes, a
trim green jacket with narrow lapels, and a buttoned-
down breast pocket.

Pamela Harte had wandered off and came back
with a darkly handsome woman in a tightly laced
green velvet bodice which was a simple display case

for mathematically round breasts, almost luminously white through the lattice. They watched the final metamorphosis of the plain man to a sophisticate with critical eyes.

The newcomer said in a plummy contralto, "It doesn't suit him at all. He's too obviously bursting with raw health. It won't do, Harry. You'll have to find him a spot in Prehistory."

Diment felt it was a little hard. He hadn't chosen it. Also, it made no sense, but nobody volunteered any explanation. Certainly it was a move in the right direction, and he reckoned that anyone fitting that chest into that green net would be wiser not to knock other people's dress.

Pamela Harte, reading his mind, said hastily, "Lydia, this is Roger Diment. Roger this is Lydia Brunswick. You look very nice. It's just that everybody has to be fitted to a particular part. I don't understand it yet. But I'm sure we're very lucky to be here."

"You can surely say that. But where is here?"

A short burly man in stage armor clanked out of the shadows. He was carrying a casque under his arm like a spare head and spoke up for action. "We've been long enough, Harry. Time to get back. They'll be all stirred up, missing these two." His eyes flicked appreciatively over Pamela's trim figure as though pointing the plain fact that she would be missed in any rational scheme.

"I reckon we should do a stint in the galleries. This time they might run a special search."

Lydia Brunswick took a deep breath which put her ancient dress under unfair strain and said slowly, "I hate to agree with George and God himself, he knows I've no wish to go into that orange routine again today, but he could be right. Give it one hour anyway. After that, I guess they'll leave it until to-morrow."

"There's just the question of whether they can be trusted." The jarring note came from a tall melancholy man in a monk's habit. Like Bedall, he was old and gray-haired, but the years seemed to have desiccated him.

Everybody looked at Bedall. Clearly he was the top hand in the organization. He said, "All right. I'll take the chance. The girl goes in the space tableau. You can take her there yourself, Geoff. Brief Andy. If there's any hint that she's a ringer, he knows what to do. I'll take Diment myself."

As the others began to move toward a door at the far end of the storeroom, he spoke directly to the new draft. "You see, I'm tender hearted. It could be the death of me. But don't believe you can get away with anything. Certain rooms are screened. Outside here always wear a hat or a wig. They've been fixed to block detectors. Yours is that white helmet, Pamela. You'll need a wig with sideburns. There it is on the peg. Okay? Let's go."

Roger Diment was glad to be sitting on a heavily upholstered settle in a large alcove dimly lit by a couple of courtesy lamps.

Unwilling to use the elevators at this time, since power loss would show up on the grid control, Bedall had taken his party up an interminable spiral stair-way to the main floors of the Museum complex. There were eight horseshoe galleries giving a blow-by-blow, chronological sneak view of the human scene from the dawn of prehistory to the twenty-ninth century.

As far as he could judge, he was on the fifth floor, halfway along the left-hand leg, and Pamela

Harte had been taken farther along the same level to her space station.

It was not uncomfortable. Fussy perhaps and cluttered for his taste, but if this was a typical twentieth-century sitting room in the European sector, it was a viable proposition for a reasonable life.

It was an oblong area eight meters by five, open to the circulation space on a long side, with a kitchenette in a recess. The open side had a waist-high bronze grille for the public to lean on in contemplation. Hand-out leaflets in a rack gave the detail. Starting with a standard warning not to damage the exhibits, they said that domestic affairs at this time were still organized on the primitive family basis, and here was a family, at home in its secluded nest, very wasteful in community resources and too inward-looking for the public good.

The floor was carpeted edge-to-edge with a thick-piled cover, which the blurb said was woven from animal fiber and was a reservoir for germs and dust. Furniture was solidly built of yellow wood. Narrow pipes ran round the skirting boards and connected large corrugated panels to a heating source. It was indeed a womb of comfort. He had to work at it to stay awake.

Four others filled out the tableau. A boy in blue jeans and a T-shirt with MIKE across the chest in Times Bold was sitting at a table upstage left, digging at some problem with an open book and a scribble pad. Bedall was sitting over across the floor, legs crossed, watching him closely. A large elderly woman in a thick tweed skirt and a pale blue jersey, with gingery hair screwed to a round bun, was upright, sitting on a high-backed chair and sewing a button on a shirt. A very slim, long-legged girl with a red skirt that fell a few centimeters below crotch level, a see-through blouse of pale blue-green, and a mass of platinum blonde hair falling to shoulder level, was standing in front of a mirror, hung on a wall behind Bedall, with an eye pencil poised for action.

Bedall said, "Not long now. We'll give it another ten minutes and then break. They're sure to check around here, but I guess they think it can wait."

"How long do you have to stay here?"

"You get used to it. There's plenty to do. At least in these literate times. You can read, walk about, talk when there isn't a visitor. We change about. A week here, then a week on another level, it's really very interesting. You bone up on social history. The Museum opens at ten hundred, closes at sixteen hundred, with a short midday break. Closed all day Saturday and Sunday. Not many visitors in fact. Attendance has dropped off steadily. Some days not one."

Diment was conscious that it was a long time since he had eaten. Now the action had cooled off, he was more than ready for a meal stop. "What about food?"

"That can be difficult. You have to watch Annie here. She's overliberal with the seasoning. We do a typical meal of the period at midday. On the pre-history level it tends to be rugged if there's an audience. You pretend to eat it. The androids shove it down anyway. One of their chores is emptying out at the end of the day. They have a disposable bag."

"How many androids are there?"

"The majority. You and I for instance are the only representatives of *Homo sapiens* in this out-fit."

"How long has this been going on?"

"Questions. Questions. You're still on probation, son. But I've been watching you and I'll use my judgment. I reckon you're what you claim to be. How old would you say I was?"

Bedall heaved himself out of his chair and began to pace about the carpet.

"I wouldn't know. Fifty, at a guess?"

"Sixty-eight this year. Thirty-eight years I've been here. Ben Gunn his own self. I started the whole thing off."

"That's a long time." Diment's mind grappled with it. Had he been wise? Maybe it was better to be phased out in his prime, than spend more years than he had yet lived in a voluntary prison.

Something of his thought was picked up shrewdly by the proprietor. "You don't like the idea. You think it would bore the pants off of you. Not so. It's gone like a flash. There's a lot to do. All interesting. We have a very good recreation area on the roof. Everything you could want. Altogether we're a hundred strong now. Anyway, where else would we be allowed to live? You name it. Under the present laws, we'd be unacceptable anywhere in the hemisphere. I've more than doubled my span and I'm not done yet. Not by a long chalk."

Without warning the circulation space flooded with light. Bedall stopped his pacing and said quietly, "Okay. This is it. Don't worry. Just be natural. React normally to anything that happens. Good luck."

He moved without haste to his original seat. Somewhere along the level an elevator grille clicked and feet clumped on the parquet.

It sounded like a large party, moving and stopping and gradually drawing nearer. When the house lights went up to full strength, only three figures appeared above the bronze barrier to peer into the nest.

All were androids. One, finished in silver gray, had an armband which said *Curator*. The other two, in gunmetal, hung about like tinkers' mules with ancillary gear, were security details, with a double helix in blue and silver on their chest consoles equipped to shoot, drug, dismember, or restrain at the drop of a hat from any historical era.

One of them lifted an oblong box with a frill of antennae and a large calibrated dial and pointed it at Annie's head. On a count of three, he said flatly, "Negative," and transferred to the blonde. "Negative."

Diment was struggling with an urge to clear his throat, which had developed a spasm as though a hair had been drawn across it. He felt that his eyes were watering and that his face had gone puce.

At the fifth "Negative," he managed a miserly breath through clenched teeth and told himself that he would make it, albeit internally ruptured at every vulnerable point.

The trio moved on. Bedall held up a large restraining hand. Not until they had put two more alcoves between them did he move quickly to the kitchenette and come in with a beaker of water.

"Well done. It's a strain at first. During the day it doesn't matter. They expect you to do all the human things, spit, fart, blow your nose, anything that seems logical at the time. But not on an off beat inspection. Mind you, this only happens when there's been an escape. They have to get special authority to crack the time lock. Normally we're safe as a vault."

Fifteen minutes later the circulation space dimmed. Bedall moved cautiously to the rail and looked out. "They're off this level. One useful limitation these gribbles have, they need a lot of light. Lidido drops right away in the shade. It's the photosynthesis bit."

He crossed to the blonde who had been working at her eye shadow in the light, but was now stuck with extended contemplation. He patted her neat can with a fatherly hand and got a low giggle. "It's a pity she's an android. Just my type. Answers to Amanda. God, before I pulled out some human company, I got so that I hardly knew the difference. There's one of those daughters of Amenophis III, in the Egyptology sector, that I used to chat up by the hour."

"What did she have to say?"

"Not much. Offered me her little unguent jar every now and then."

"How long before you had a companion?"

"Three years to the day. I moved real slow. Worked out the detail. Learned a lot about the setup. When I was ready, I started at the top. Fixed the head curator. They're all modified now. We've nothing to fear from the local staff. Just these security monkeys who come in from time to time. And the public, of course. You can never be sure a smart Aleck isn't going to nip over the fence with some sadistic ploy."

A strip light over the cooker in the kitchenette blinked on and off. Diment looked his question. The oracle said, "That's it. We can wrap it up there. Visitors gone."

"How do you know that?"

"Not so fast. I think you're what you claim to be; but you want to know too much. And I talk too much. I guess I'm still compensating for all the silent time. Let's go."

It was too dark to see much detail, but Diment reckoned they passed a fair cross-section of Everyday Life at the Beginning of the Technological Revolution. He identified a schoolroom, a business office with a typist on an executive knee, a factory corner, a farmyard with animals and dung bouquet, and a chapel with a file of stationary choir boys in procession.

Pamela's space station must have been on the other leg of the horseshoe, because she met them at the elevator trunk, gleaming whitely out of the murk and attended by a long, hatchet-faced man also in white.

Bedall said, "Well, Andy. How did it go?"

Even in a dim light it was clear enough that the spaceman kept all ripples of emotion off his face. He opened his mouth a bare centimeter as a concession and aired a grievance for starters. "It's not good enough Harry. It could a' bin verra nasty. No time to brief the girl at all. We canna afford to go for these sudden whims. It needs plannin'. You've always said that yourself."

"You managed all right."

"Aye, but I don't like it. It only needs once. Just once and the cover's gone."

"I understand that. Is she all right?"

"Aye. I had her on the truth machine while we were waitin' for the clear. She's a rare flibberty gibbert, but she's no spy. She wouldna have the savvy for that kind of work."

Pamela Harte cleared her ringlet from her left shoulder with an impatient flick. Gratitude had its limits, she was tired of the lay figure role. She said, "I had a very difficult assignment. He put me in an excursion module with a very fresh android that kept putting its hand on my knee. You couldn't see it from your command capsule. If we'd been stuck there another two minutes I'd have been fighting him off—"

She stopped and peered into the gloom over Andy's shoulder. Then she skipped smartly behind Diment. "That's the one. It's got malevolent eyes."

Bedall said, "That's no android. It's Russ Gribbin. You must be out of your mind, Andy, putting her with Russ. He's only got one good idea in his head. Well, let it rest there. Up top. Get some rest. Tomorrow is another busy day."

Roger Diment was glad of his narrow bed. Bedall had promised something better when a working party could get at it, but even a temporary shakedown was more than he could have expected. He told himself that he who has nothing may sleep. But sleep did not immediately take over.

There was a lot to think about. He was toward the far end of a long room, which had been divided off into living units. He had been impressed by the ingenuity and organization behind it.

When the group had gathered from every level, they had gone to work by numbers. This space, under the very eaves, might have been destined for an extra gallery. It was all of a hundred meters long by forty athwartships. Lightweight acoustic screens had been run out from storage bays. Beds had appeared from the wall face. Food, cooked earlier in the day, when the power could be taken without check, was lifted from vacuum containers still piping hot. The empty garret became a thriving long house in full social swing.

Social grouping was very flexible. Contemplatives of either sex could have a single alcove, there was an all-male dormitory sector and an all-female dormitory sector. Located toward the center, there was a belt of two-bed accommodation for those building up permanent relationships.

It was all very seemly and worked out with the minimum of direction. But without tacit agreement in the system, it would not work at all. Bedall had every right to be proud of the colony he had founded and to be anxious to preserve it intact.

Meals could be taken at any one of four centers along the complex. Each one had something different to offer. Bedall explained that supplies were geared to present typical dishes from any age, and they usually chose four to cover all tastes.

Diment had settled for a twentieth-century gourmet's dish of ground pork, bound between alternate slices of thin beef and seethed in a pot with bouquet garni, tomatoes, and mushrooms. Complemented by a carafe of red wine and rounded off by a large wedge of traditional pie with a strange sweet sauce, it had reduced him to bemused silence. Fed for years on simulates, he reckoned his journey had been worth the trouble, even if he did not survive the night.

Pamela Harte, despairing of getting any conversation at all from him, had been driven to make peace with Russ Gribbin, who had sidled purposefully into the empty seat on her left.

Except that he kept shoving his knee against her leg, he was reasonably passive, his hands being busy with the main chore. It was, however, on all counts, a lot better than being dead. The wine in any case made her feel lightheaded and disinclined to struggle.

He was on about his last assignment in a Babylonian tableau. "They had a saying that in paradise the ittudi bird utters not the cry of the ittudi bird."

"Is that good?"

"It depends on what the cry of the ittudi bird was like."

It figured. He was not all bad. She gave him a beaming smile and regretted it as he shifted his chair closer.

Bedall had given Diment and Pamela an empty alcove for the night, but explained that they would have to make up their minds whether or not they wanted to stay together. He had said, "It's not like outside. You can't have a free-for-all in a working community. It leads to all kinds of trouble. After tonight, we'll fix rooms in the big dormitories. If you want to go into partnership, that's okay. But think about it and be sure. There's a ceremony to mark the occasion and everybody knows about it. Don't rush into it. We've got to have stability here or somebody's going to do the wrong thing and blow the cover."

Diment raised himself on one elbow and looked across a five-meter gap to where Pamela Harte was sleeping. She was turned toward him with her ringlet luminously dark on the white cover. Oval face, small straight nose, lips open. Breathing heavily at that. Interesting, though. He had never been so interested in another human being.

Twenty-four hours ago on the island, the huge Wayfarers' party had been going with a frenetic swing. He could remember a large brown girl with a chest that must have crossed the thousand milli-meter Rubicon, swaying toward him with arms straight out from the shoulder palms uppermost, fingers open wide.

Did she in fact make it? That was the last clear input to his data acquisition network. After that there was a jumble of sight, sound, and sensation, giving way finally to the hard surface of the conveyer tray and the pressure of the band round his eyes.

How had it been done? Something in the drink was the likely one. Everybody had a drink. That was a common denominator with the androids circling endlessly and seeing that nobody stayed away from a loaded tray for long. Come to think of it, there had been groups of people about who were complete strangers. Present in the flesh, but not committed to the action. Voyeurs.

On the other hand, it had to be selective at some point. There must have been over four thousand milling about on the island. Well, with everybody out cold they could work through the identity serials and take their pick. Some groups would take a bit of unraveling at that.

He found himself wondering what Pamela Harte had been doing when the bell tolled. Currently, she looked as though she had never joined a maenad rout.

Better not enquire too closely into the past, his own or anybody else's. Against all statistical likelihood he had been given the chance to start over. The future was not bound to the past. Not necessarily. There was some possibility of changing direction.

He saw with a force like revelation that he was right at the heart of the weakness in the system. While there was life there was a chance of change. Without the prospect of changing the future by his own effort, a man was a piece of period furniture. The human situation had to be dynamic. Forward or backward, but never standing still. By fixing the pattern, they had been forced to put in the artificial stop at the Wayfarer stage. Otherwise there would be too much time for analysis. Revolutions were made by the old. The young only shouted the slogans.

Pamela's calm face was an affront. He wanted to shake her awake, ask her if she had noticed anything, have her listen to his theory. Then he was hearing a subdued buzzer behind his head and the long room was full of natural light.

Bedall with his tufts of hair in a vertical fizz was stalking in saying, "Another day, another life. Out of that sack, Diment, there's a lot to do in the next hour."

CHAPTER THREE

Looked at in natural light, with the edge of wonder blunted by use, there was less glamor on the set. Faces looked a lot older. Many were not at their best in the morning hour.

Diment, earning his breakfast by pushing screens away into their slots, could see that the equipment was showing signs of hard wear. Bedall's empire had a strict limit. Its resources were finite. Food for the morning meal had to be simple. There was a mixed cereal porridge on the cool side, lukewarm coffee, slices of soda bread.

A starving peasant would have jumped about with little glad cries, but the company was too far over the bread line for gratitude.

He was helping a round-faced, plump man already dressed as a harem keeper, who introduced himself as Joe Brogan and let him know that there were some who thought Bedall was too high-handed.

"It wouldn't do a scrap of harm to rig up a cooking range and put something on a man could get his teeth into. It's a couple of hours before the doors open and there's not been any visitor across the lobby before eleven for as long as I remember. But no, Lord God almighty says not. He won't alter a thing. You'll see, when you've been here a spell. It's a bloody dictatorship. What did you do outside?"

"I was a gunnery specialist. For the Central Wirral Stadium. Athletics on the side. There's a lot of interest in hand guns. Externalizes aggression, the mind-benders say. When I left, there were forty in the section, running the ranges, maintaining the weapons. I liked it."

"Not much scope for that here. And if there was, Bedall wouldn't want to know. I was in electronics myself. I could fix this place so that no android could reach this level. Then we could cut all this lash-up-and-stow caper; but Bedall won't hear of it. But there'll come a time when some of us can't carry on with a normal day's program. What then? This area should be sealed off and ready for occupation all day." Diment was shocked. The frailty of age was not a concept he had ever encountered. A new boy, he kept silent.

When the garret was clear and swept, Bedall held a short briefing for the assembled company. In the mass they were as bizarre a group as ever stood together. Chaldean chest joy, heavy with lapis lazuli and carnelian, glittered brazenly beside the sober black habit of a Sister of Mercy. Roman greaves followed cross garters. Powdered perukes towered over balding pates with rakish chaplets of plastic olive leaves.

Diment stood with Pamela at the back and reckoned they had been lucky with their first assignment.

Reading from an order board with a clip, and passing one hand in a smoothing action over the hairless center of his head, Director Bedall said, "No changes today. You know the drill. It's just possible there may be another check; that has happened before after a break. That shouldn't worry anybody. Evening meal from Pepys's London, Tenth-Century China, Twentieth-Century Spain and Twenty-fourth-Century Ireland—for a laugh. Any questions?"

Whatever the size of Joe Brogan's faction, there were none. The revue company filed out with a rising decibel level of chat as they adjusted to another interesting day at culture's coal face.

Pamela Harte lingered outside Diment's station. It was not just unwillingness to join Gribbin in his capsule; there was something eerie about the whole complex which unsettled her.

Bedall had gone off on a tour of inspection. They were alone, standing at the barrier like two regular visitors.

Annie had stopped sewing her shirt and had gone on to another part of her program. She was cleaning house. She was pushing a three-wheeled vacuum cleaner with a dust bag over the carpet, methodically moving chairs to get a clear run.

Mike had shifted his books and was oiling a bat, using a rag and a bottle of dark linseed oil. His mother was grumbling at him and telling him he ought to do it in the yard. Amanda was still at her mirror, but had stripped off to a basic minimum of triangular, eau-de-nil briefs with matching equalizer and was drying her hair with a hand blower.

Pamela Harte said, "I can't put it properly into words. But what have we got that they haven't got? How do we know that we're the humans and they're the androids? It's uncanny. I feel like an interloper. And how do we know what they get up to when we leave? They have what the Western World was always going on about."

"What's that?"

"Immortality. Going on doing what you've been doing forever. This shows it up for what it is. A nonsense."

"You're looking at it with a jaundiced eye. It isn't the same thing at all. They don't *feel* what they're doing. They don't enjoy it."

"I don't know that I'm going to enjoy fending off that Gribbin for the rest of the day. Look at that. She's *listening* to me."

The girl had stopped the drier and had turned to look at the audience. There was some force in Bedall's argument. She was a honey. Mouth open, she was miming delight like a model in a detergent ad.

Diment said, "Don't worry. It's all strange, but we haven't seen much of it yet. Give it a chance. I'll talk to Bedall. He'll fix you up with something smoochy in the Eastern line. Get into diaphanous harem pants and you'll feel a new woman. See you later on."

He was over the barrier, a zealous workman, but she did not go. She said, "Of course, you can hardly wait to get near that skinny zombie. She'll be a big disappointment, I can tell you that. At least Gribbin knows the difference."

Her hands were still on the rail and Diment held them there. Before she could take any avoiding action, he had leaned over and kissed her mouth. Anemone soft, a surprised O.

There was a moment of balance, a suspension of disbelief; then Amanda gave her general-purpose giggle. Pamela Harte snatched her hands free and set off up the horseshoe without a backward look.

Diment clanked somberly along the third level at the tail end of the homeward rush. It had been a busy week, but he reckoned he had gotten a neck lock on the system. Bedall had the right of it. There was no reason why the Community should not sweat it out for as long as they wanted to keep life bubbling in the pot. Well, simmering.

He was armed cap-à-pie in black body armor with a beak-like casque surmounted by a green plume. It should have made him feel three meters tall, but by isolating him from his surroundings it was leading to negative thinking and introspection.

Somewhere inside the ironware he was alive, but to what purpose? Going through the motions of a fourteenth-century day was basically the same as his first stint in the twentieth, or the intermediary bit as an early American tycoon in a stove-pipe hat. Culture patterns changed the detail, but human anatomy and physiology were the changeless, underlying strata on which the species stood firm. Even his own sophisticated era had the same basic drives. Except one. He stood still in the corridor to think about that one.

Personal survival. Everywhere along the line, they had hung on to life under all the rigors that age, pain, penury, and humiliation could lay on. They were dragged, protesting to the last against the injustice of it, to a reluctant grave. But his century went like lambs to the slaughter, well before their time. How had that come about? Not by natural choice for a certainty.

He clumped on to the stairhead. Bedall was right to insist that they keep the day's costume ready for a quick scatter to location in emergency; but it was rough on some. He reckoned he was shifting forty kilograms of dead weight over the ground.

Leaning on the elevator housing for a breather, he watched the flow with a jaundiced eye. Then Pamela Harte appeared from a lower level and there was some justification for the system.

First in vision was a wig of intensely black hair, set in a mass of tight plaits which hung to her bare shoulders and gave her skin the pallor of alabaster. Heavy gold bracelets underlined the satisfying roundness of her arms. Eyes were huge, elongated, and made brilliant by turquoise shadow. A sketchy robe of semitransparent white linen clung snugly to every body curve. It was enough to cause a mass breakout from the sarcophagi, and he checked down the stair to see if any gaunt figure with trailing bandages was lurching in pursuit. But there was only Gribbin in a green tunic, red tights, turned up shoes, and a liripipe hat.

Since the visor was hinged back, Pamela recognized the piece of statuary. She had not seen much of him during the week. True to his word, Bedall had fixed them each a niche in the single sex dormitories. It promoted leisure for thought, and one of her conclusions had been that if he wanted her, he would have to make an effort and seek her out.

This was against the pattern of the society they had left, where a brisk free-for-all put the initiative on either side of the sex line, without prejudice; but it seemed more natural. There was time to play hard to get. For, as a Roman colleague had recently said, "Venus hates haste."

She was all set to sweep past, palms flattened front and rear as in a mural, when a mailed arm closed the gap. Diment said hollowly, "There you are, then. What have you been getting up to?"

At the same time he pulled her out of the stream

of traffic and motioned Gribbin to carry on up the shaft. That one slowed, fingered his crook, judged that he was out of his technological class, and went on. The look in his eye said plainly that he would wait his time.

Diment said unfairly, "I can't understand what you see in that one. He's a five-star creep."

"If you only want to say that, I'm surprised you waited for me."

"I didn't wait for you. This suit weighs a ton. I was resting my feet."

"It's been a long day. I'll be glad to get upstairs. Do you feel rested enough to move on?"

Diment switched to basics. The change in tone was clear enough even from his personal acoustic cowl. "What do you make of it, Pamela? Can you settle for this?"

"There isn't much choice, is there? In the literature where I am now, there's a whole lot about a character called Ma'at, daughter of the sun god, featured with a green plume like the one you have, though the likeness stops there."

"So?"

"Ma'at allows a man or woman to strive after every excellence, until there is no fault left in his nature. Keep in tune with Ma'at to learn the good life of harmony, justice, and truth that holds the world together."

"So?"

"So the pursuit of Ma'at can take place anywhere. You don't need space. Only yourself and your attitudes."

"And you reckon we can work on that for the next fifty years, give or take a decade?"

"I don't know. I'm just reporting an interesting bit

from the archives. If Ma'at looked like that Amanda, you'd be on to it like a hound dog."

Diment give his casque an exasperated knock with the palm of his gauntlet. The hole in his helmet fell shut with a definitive snap. His answer was lost and sounded muffled to his own ears. By the time he had stopped a passing blacksmith to knock it free with his hammer, she was round the twist of the spiral.

When he finally lumbered into the long house, there was enough going on to deflect the personal issue altogether. A start had been made on the scene shifting chore, but now it had stopped dead, and it looked like a transit camp in a disaster area. The whole community had gathered in a ragged mob in the center. Bedall had both arms raised in a mime for quiet. When he got it, Diment's heavy tread was the only ongoing sound, and every eye tracked him to the fringe. As he ground to a halt, Bedall had another go.

He said, "Easy all. Not so fast. You're jumping to a whole lot of conclusions. I'll hear what Carol has to say and we'll have a regular meeting about it after supper. I've heard a lot of rumors in my time and mostly they come to nothing. Now just carry on fixing for supper. We'll all think better after a meal and a rest. What do you say?"

It was a good hour before Carol Greer took the stand and the mood had mellowed. Optimism had grown on a full stomach, and Diment conceded that Bedall had picked up a fair knowledge of the group mind. There were even a few approving whistles as she left her place and walked twenty meters to the high table where Bedall had gathered his organizing committee.

Chairs had been brought from all parts and arranged in a crescent. Bedall had Lydia Brunswick on his left and George Orman on his right. Farther out on the wings, Geoff Konstad, a melancholy man, and Andy Granger completed the inner wheel, a rough bunch for anybody to face without a good story.

Carol Greer was a fairly recent addition to the cell and could have been plucked from the disposal line on a statistics kick. For comfortable dining, she had discarded a chatelaine's conical hat with a veil and a complicated metal belt, and appeared in a basic white shift, which went into free fall from the jut of a thousand-millimeter bust.

Two tight coils of honey-colored hair sited over each ear insulated her to some extent from her public, and she was wearing the fixed ingratiating smile of one partially deaf, but anxious to please. Bedall rapped on the table top with a gavel to get quiet.

He said, "Now we'll hear what Carol has to say. If we all get it straight from the horse's mouth, to coin a phrase, there won't be any distorted version going the rounds." He passed his hand in a smoothing motion over the bald area of his head and called the principal witness, using a quiet, fatherly tone to give her confidence. "Now Carol. You tell them what you told me."

"Pardon me. What did you say?"

Bedall, a practical man, leaned across and lifted one of the ear muffs. "Tell them all about it."

"Oh. Yes, of course. Well it's very simple, really. I was playing that scene in the keep, where Sir Persimmon fastens me in that belt and then throws the key in the moat. And by the way, I want a change tomorrow, or a change in Sir Persimmon. I don't know how Russ Gribbin got that part."

Orman, still in a monk's habit, shifted irritably in his stall. "Get on with it, Carol. We'll be here all night."

"What did you say?"

"Oh, my God. Forget it."

Carol Greer shrugged eloquently, dismissing the celibate to his own private world of muddle, and went on, "He walks off to some Holy War and I walk about wringing my hands. Well, there were two or three visitors at the barrier and I went just about a meter off so they could have a good look at my ball and chain, as it says in the script. Well, there were these two, and honestly I couldn't tell you whether they were androids or whatever, but when I turned round, one of them leaned right over and slapped at me. I bet I have a blue bruise the size of a plate, because I mark ever so easily."

There was a reflective pause. She had set the scene well and Diment believed that such a dedicated artiste would add corroborative detail by showing the site in full color, but she picked up the thread of her tale.

"Well, I turned round and gave them a look and said that bit about not touching the exhibits. One of them said, 'You'd swear they were flesh and blood. I'll bet she has the duplicate key to that contraption round her neck on a thong. I've half a mind to borrow that one and leave it in Arthur's bed. That'd make him think.' The other one said, 'I wouldn't do that even to an android. What do you reckon they'll do to this lot when the place is closed down?' Well you can imagine, I just stood and *stared* at them."

There was a general buzz of chat from the audience and Bedall had to knock again. When there was quiet, he asked, "Was that all? Was that all they said?"

"No. They were walking away with their backs to me. So I followed as far as I could along the barrier. I lifted my hair up like this so that I could hear better."

Carol, with a small dramatic gesture that carried conviction, put both hands to her coiled plaits and shoved them out horizontal, revealing glowing pink ears and giving her magnificent figure a taut line.

Holding the pose, she carried on. "The first one, mean-looking with a narrow head, said, 'Mostly they'll go to the Regional History Park in Shropshire. Any they don't want will be scrapped. Could happen this year. I've seen the plans for a stadium on this site.' Then they were looking at the Early Printing sequence next door and I couldn't hear any more. Also, a school party came up and a very forward child said, 'How can that lady do a tinkle with that metal thing fastened on?' So I made a dignified exit into the solar."

It all had the ring of truth. She had heard what she had heard. There was silence from all hands.

Bedall said slowly, "Thank you, Carol. You'd better leave one ear open for a time. Does anybody want to ask a question?"

There was none from the body of the hall. Andy Granger, a difficult man to convince, said half-heartedly, knowing he was fighting a rearguard against conviction, "Who was in the printin' section? Did they see these two?"

A small man in the second row, still wearing an ink-daubed smock, stood up. "I saw them."

"Did you hear anythin'?"

"It's not possible. There's the clack of that machine. You hardly know whether there's visitors about or not. But I did see the two of them. They just stayed a minute and went on."

Bedall said, "I don't think we can dispute it. In any case it wouldn't be sensible to ignore it. There are the facts. New to me and new to you. I'm only surprised there's been no hint of it before. You'd think there would have been official inventories taken and checks made on the use the place gets. Maybe they just don't want to know. For the most part there won't be a bleep out of citizens' council. A stadium would be rated as an advantage."

Diment looked round the group. It was a lot to take in. In some ways the direct confrontation was worse than rumor, which had emotional overtones and could be discounted. Previous experience in the city, where personal decisions were hardly ever taken, was no preparation. Even here, Bedall had set up as a comfortable father figure. But they were thinking about it.

Across the floor Pamela Harte got to her feet, a worthy scion of the Middle Kingdom. She said, "This must be worse for Harry than anybody. He's put a whole lot of work into this enterprise. We owe him a lot. I wouldn't have missed this last week for anything. One thing I know. When you have time to consider it, you understand that the system outside is all wrong. I don't want to die and I don't believe I should have to accept it for a long time yet. Outside, the pace is stepped up until you don't stop to analyze what's going on. Even then, there'd be objections if there wasn't something working for the system. We're brainwashed into taking it. How is it done? Can anybody tell me that?"

George Orman on the platform had heard enough. "That's hardly the question. We'd be here all night if

we start debating about outside. You should rule
that out of order, Harry."

A chairman given a compliment is always slow
to slap down a speaker. Bedall, anyway, was prepared for a little lateral thinking. He said, "It's an
interesting point. But I wouldn't know the answer.
I only know that I only began to think for myself when I got here. I guess there must be something to it. Like George, however, I have to say
that it doesn't go any way to solving our problem."

Diment found himself speaking out without any
prepared speech, but wanting to support a trier.
"Pamela has something there." There was a brisk
"Right!" from Gribbin, but not much enthusiasm
elsewhere. Some faces said plainly that people new
to the enclave should keep quiet until they knew
the score. Diment pressed on with, "If we think
back we must come up against that. Now where is
the chief difference? The food is a special catering
job to make up the period dishes. Water comes
straight in from the distillation plant. No additives
there. It wouldn't occur to anybody that it was
necessary, because there isn't a resident human staff.
Hasn't been for ages. That could be one thing.
Also, by wearing screening in the head gear, we cut
out any direct suggestion broadcasts that might be
going out."

Bedall could accept a digression from a female
fan, but thought Diment was taking it too far. His
gavel was in midair when Lydia Brunswick put a
restraining hand on his arm. "Not so fast, Harry.
Let him finish. There might just be an angle that
helps us. What do you mean by broadcasts? I never
heard of it."

Diment felt that he was being forced into a
corner. He wanted to be another questioner, and

was being expected to produce a program. But he was thinking more clearly than any time he could remember. "I've no evidence for that, but the technique was standard in the twenty-second century. Every community had its own social stability center. Subliminal broadcasts went out at night. Something like group hypnosis, urging them to keep the peace and be kind to the cat. It was the only thing that finally gave the knock to the thuggery that was rife in the twenty-first. Who's to say that it hasn't been revived, with a new brief to sell acceptance of the short lifespan and the artificial Wayfarer stage at thirty?"

Andy Granger said, "Very interestin'. How did you come by that information? I never heard of it. It isn't in the handouts for that period and I've done many a long stint in the twenty-first. Beside, if it *was* so, we'd get the message here like everybody else, and we'd feel the same way."

It was a good point and Diment could sense that he was losing support. There were many nods and some satisfaction. As a newcomer, he was speaking out of turn.

Support came unexpectedly from Pamela. Long unused, her computer was having a field day. She was rapidly turning into an intellectual giant. She said, "What does it matter where Roger got the information? It makes sense. They wouldn't beam a program on the museum. They'd concentrate on the tower blocks where the dormitory areas are. Probably there's a built-in circuit. The residents would be the last to know or care. How does it help us?"

It was a good question and Diment had spent his minute's grace in finding an answer. He heard himself say, "If we do nothing, we're finished anyway.

There is a chance that we could wake up the general public to the real situation. It needs planning, but two or three ideas come to mind straight away. For a start we could take a look at the next Wayfarer party. Suppose they were all to stay awake to the end? There'd be some trouble getting them on the conveyer. Then somebody could look at this broadcast system, if it exists, and stop it. That would lead to some independent thought. With enough public confusion going on, there'd be a hold-up in major building programs. As I recall, the next Wayfarer affair is in a week's time. To make progress, I'll volunteer for that. A big group would be noticed, but another two would be a help."

The movement from simple discussion to positive forward planning had been sudden. Some of the older people looked bewildered. They had settled to a routine which they expected would see out their time. All they wanted was to be left alone to contemplate their navels. In some ways, they were as much in blinkers as the under-thirties, who were kept bemused by exploitation of the senses. The dichotomy of body and mind was complete. Those with a vigorous body had no mind to direct it, and those with a burgeoning mind had no freedom of body to support it.

The balance was out of kilter. Diment, looking round, had a moment's pessimism. This was no ginger group to set the world right. They were bucking a system that was solid, for all he knew, throughout the hemisphere.

Then he caught Pamela Harte's eye across the room. Millennia past, people had looked like that. Ma'at. Order, justice, and truth that holds the world together and allows a man to hold himself together.

They had to try. He had been given a second run at the data and he had to go wherever reason led him.

Pamela Harte, a variant of Everyman, said "I'll go with you." Three places along the row, the blacksmith Carl Borsey, who had courteously knocked up Diment's visor, a massive, barrel-chested man with a short, pointed beard, said, "I'll go along. He has the right of it. We have no choice."

Bedall took them down to the service tunnel himself. The spiral stairway in the elevator trunk went on into the basement, where the whole mass of the museum complex was carried on squat octagonal piers that split the area into an endless maze. Small roof ports almost a hundred meters apart gave a dim light. But for the most part they walked in deep shadow.

Pamela Harte said nervously, "How did you find your way into this place, or out of it for that matter?'

"I didn't come this way. I got into the museum from outside like a regular visitor. It was a year or two before I took a look down here. I knew the conveyer terminal was somewhere near. Look at the pillars as we go. You'll see a small cross marked shoulder high. Keep that on your right hand. Or left hand coming back. You can lose direction. Particularly in the dark. I was caught once in a power failure. Stuck for half a day. Thought I'd bought it."

It was said as a fact, but Diment could understand what it must have meant at the time. Bedall had played a difficult hand. He was entitled to a lot of respect.

The outlet was a narrow panel that had been fixed to swivel on a center pin. Anything else might have been found in a search of the cellar. Movement was stiff enough to withstand any casual pressure. Bedall stood with his ear to it for a full minute before he said, "All clear," and shoved it open with his shoulder.

In the corridor, he said, "Take a good look at the way back. You might need it in a hurry. It's the fifth panel from the bend. Count them along so that you know. But I'll trust you not to use it if you can be seen. They always check the museum, but they've nothing positive to go on. If they knew about this, they'd really take it apart. Good luck, anyway. Maybe this is for the best in the long term."

Bedall stuck out his hand. Diment said, "Thanks, Harry. All the work you've put in doesn't deserve to fail. We'll do what we can."

The three set off in silence, Pamela Harte in the middle, Carl Borsey on her right, Diment on her left. They were in white coveralls with the maintenance service flash on the epaulettes.

Diment had the weight of a small hand gun in his hip pocket. He had picked it from a showcase together with a sample clip of six shells. It was not much, but probably one up on his iron bar.

Now they were actually moving out on the mission, he realized the serious gaps in the brief. He was off with a toothpick to tickle up Leviathan. He must have been out of his mind to suggest it. But he was in the command slot. The others were stepping out with every misplaced confidence.

Without a weight on his back, the distance seemed shorter. Before he expected it, they were at the entrance behind the presiding computer in the conveyer terminal.

On hands and knees, Diment eased the door a

centimeter at a time. Pamela Harte, suddenly pale as a tile, flattened herself emotionally to the wall.

A patient android, standing in the narrow alley between the computer banks, snapped into life and spat a charge of serum chest high through the opening.

Diment, motivated at a basic level where reason had no part, dived forward like any frog and grabbed for its ankles with the door swinging shut at his back.

CHAPTER FOUR

Even as he moved, Roger Diment realized that he was a novice at the aggressive game. He ought to have known that the last escape, with two androids written off, would shove the establishment into counter action. It cost nothing to leave a zombie stationed at the entrance.

A further racing thought told him there was a flaw somewhere in the argument, and as his hands touched the metal legs dead ahead, he saw with rare clarity what it was. If the android was programmed to fire as the door opened he might hit anybody, friend or not.

Even leaving aside the proposition that an android's friends were thin on the ground, it was a hazard his own side would not accept. So, in spite of first appearances, there was another entrance to the terminal which was used by the organizing genius of the place.

Satisfaction in having thought it through was likely to be all the pleasure he was going to get. The android rocked back at a balance-defying angle, with its arms flailing every which way. A gyro-stabilizer cut in and held it steady. Its serum-shooting index finger began to track round for a target it could not miss again.

Diment was on his knees, arms locked round the smooth calves straining to lift with muscles corded and sweat running suddenly into his eyes. There was a flurry at his back and adhesion broke. The gyro went into a whine of overload as the android's feet were plucked from the deck.

The elementary mechanics of it sprawled Diment flat on his back, with a view of the android's boot soles as it took off in uninhibited flight. It cleared the barrier in a low trajectory and disappeared from sight.

Carl Borsey, whose weighty charge had tripped the balance, stumbled to the rail to see it land on its dome. Pamela Harte knelt in womanly concern beside the bemused weightlifter, who was sitting up.

He said, "Where did it go?"

Then he was struggling to his feet, expecting a rush from all sides. But except for an echo from the single thud and the ongoing whine of the gyro, there was quiet on the set.

Borsey said, "Only look at that. You'd think the bastard was human."

They lined the bar beside him. The long hall was as it had been at the end of the last operational phase. The conveyer was stopped and its attendants were at their stations waiting for the call. Nothing moved. The android was balancing cleverly on its dented casque with its arms stretched out and its gyro leg at the vertical like any acrobat earning his keep.

Diment said, "Load it on to the conveyer beyond the last work head. Then if the line moves it'll be delivered into the furnace."

When it was folded into a tray, still vibrating

in a simulacrum of a stunned man, they felt like ghouls. Pamela Harte said, "Will it *feel* anything?"

Borsey said shortly, "We can only hope so. What's now, chief?"

"Along the tunnel. See where it makes out."

They went in single file, Diment ahead, Pamela in the middle. It was a long, silent trek and a good half hour before the level took a slope up and they were climbing toward the island.

Unfamiliar with traditional procedure as leader of a war party, Diment stopped suddenly without holding up his hand, and Pamela Harte, who was going along head down, watching for the support ribs that littered the deck, blundered pneumatically into his back.

Her mouth was open for a legitimate beef, but she was near enough for him to grab her ringlet and whip it round as a gag. "Quiet. Do you hear anything?"

Unable to speak, she had to roll her eyes and nod, but Borsey, trailing three meters on the incline, hissed back, "Following up the pipe."

Diment had his hand gun out and was staring down a clear run to the point where the change in level appeared to seal the tunnel. There was a growing murmur and a vibration underfoot, as though a trolley was racing toward them.

There was nothing to see, but there was a definite sense of something approaching at speed. Roof ports dimmed in succession. A drop in the note to a rising growl told that a motor had gone on load to take the slope.

Then it was past with a wow and withdrawing ahead.

Pamela Harte, having cleared her gag and filing

the insult for future reference, said uncertainly, "What was that, then?"

Borsey was looking at the shape of the conduit and Diment had it before he could speak. "Of course. We only saw one entrance and we didn't look for another. This is only a quarter of a circle. There could be three other channels. One below this to take the conveyer back, two more at the side. There'll be a shuttle for personnel. And a supply line, I shouldn't wonder. That'll be the managerial staff going to take charge of the exercise."

Ten minutes later they were facing another flexible flap that sealed the mouth of the tunnel and divided the quick from the dead.

Diment lay flat on the conveyer and looked through a two-centimeter gap. There was no doubt it was a marshaling area. Long tables flanked the conveyer. Rows of push trolleys, each with an attendant android, stood waiting for the dead line.

Left of where he was and curving from a point which was out of sight, but somewhere close at hand, a shining monorail on single pillar supports ran the length of the hall and disappeared at the far end round a twist.

Pamela Harte's hazel eyes, almost all pupil, were full of questions. He said shortly, "This is it. We can't afford to trigger off an alarm. Slowly out. Move left. There's a rail. I reckon if we walk along it, we won't be noticed. Okay?"

Outside the curtain, they stood still for a count of five. No android shifted a millimeter. Diment sized it up carefully and jumped for the bar, hauling himself up in a smooth heave. Then he lay along it and held his hands for the girl.

It was half a meter broad on its top surface, narrowing to a flange that carried the running gear for the shuttles. Rock solid. Walking along, they had an overall view of the dispatch department. It was clinically clean and set out in the best principles of time and motion. Wayfarers could be processed without a misspent erg.

Borsey said, "What about heaving a rock through that computer panel. Give the little tin bastards something to worry about?"

The same thought had struck Diment, but the mantle of organizer had brought caution as a free extra. "Not at this time. Nothing to put the finger on this entrance. I want them to think we came across with the regular guests."

Pamela Harte said indignantly, *"Guests?* Victims. Innocents going to the slaughter. How could we be so dumb? Look at that. They've even got bins marked up for small valuable items. I bet my other earring went into one of those."

Borsey said, "You're lucky they didn't take your other ear. Nice adjustment, that."

As the line curved out of the main hall, Diment signaled for a stop. Then he went forward alone, edging along until he could just see round the twist. Fifty meters on a shuttle was drawn up to an offloading bay. There was a broad platform on its right with an elevator trunk recessed in the rear wall. Beyond the shuttle the tunnel was closed by a silver-gray bulkhead. The commuters had not hung about. There was nobody in sight.

On the platform, Diment read off the legend on an indicator. They were not at rock bottom. One floor below was labeled *Freight*. Borsey was probably right. A lower section of the tunnel was used to shift supplies. Up the funnel there was a choice of twenty stops with ground level five up and Demographer at the top of the heap.

He tried to visualize the island. It was maybe a kilometer on its long axis facing the shore and perhaps a kilometer across. Buildings covered all the center in a continuous mass. Mostly low. There was only one that stood out as a high-rise block. That was the tower core in the center with a revolving beacon mounted on its penthouse roof to flash out a cheerful message of goodwill to the empty sea.

So they were likely to be directly underneath the hub. The organizers ran the system from here.

His mind went off on a brief, free-wheeling trip. It was unbelievable that the human crop should have gotten itself in this pass. With a new sense of History, after the time in the museum, it seemed utterly unlikely that all the thrustful effort over the millennia should have petered out into a static situation. But then, looking back, he had accepted it himself without question. Personal identity had never been an issue. From way back, he had always been one of a group, busy on a group activity, every satisfaction, from eating to sex, organized on a group basis. Even the last lemming migration of Wayfarers was carried through by group dynamics with nobody standing up and shouting, "This is happening to me, Roger Diment, heir to half a million years of evolution."

Borsey said, "Well chief?"

They were both looking at him. That was part of the answer. There was a built-in tendency to accept leadership. They would follow anything with a program, even a few kilograms of old iron tarted up with scientific jargon, even as unprotected peasants had followed an elaborate figure in armor and been cut down in swathes for their gullibility, or fledgling chicks would follow a cat.

True, all true; but none of it absolved him from

making a decision. He left it to his own biological computer, that unconscious agent of the life force, and it said for him, "We'll be more effective and less noticed if we split up. I'll go up top and take a look at the *Demographer*. Carl, you stop off at level three and see what goes on in the cellar. Pamela, take the kitchen on the ground floor. You're looking for additives that they slip into the drink and the food. If possible, find out where they come from. Stop the supply for the party."

Pamela Harte said, "Where do we meet and when?"

"Down here. Twenty-four hundred hours on the nose. Get over to the conveyer tunnel and wait just inside the flap. After that time don't hang about. Make your own way back."

"Suppose we fail and the conveyer is being used?"

"There's always another day. The important thing is that somebody's awake at last. Pick out one you like the look of and bring him along to join the minstrel troupe."

Borsey peeled off the stick with a laconic "See you." The landing area at the *Cellar* stop was open to a long hall with rows of barrels on cradles, bottle racks, crates, and vats. There was a heady alcoholic bouquet as the hatch slid back and they saw him breathe deeply in appreciation. He was a round peg in a round hole. Personnel selection had been right on the nose.

Two general-purpose androids stove-enameled bright yellow, took advantage of the stop and stepped smartly into the cage. One of them pushed the selector for level twelve, then they both switched to Non Op to conserve libido.

At ground level there was less enthusiasm from the appointed agent. Her quick intake of breath as the cage slid silently to a stop, owed nothing to the grille. But she went out with her shoulders square and a firm step, trim and capable; a small human gesture that touched Diment's heart.

At level twelve, there was little to see, with a small reception area and four sets of swing doors leading off. The androids slipped into gear and moved away. Diment might have been invisible for all the notice they took.

At the terminus, he was in executive country; deep-pile blue carpet and gold-plated door pulls. There was a choice of three exits, lying behind a low dividing wall set out with a variety of house plants and pierced by a wicket gate. The landing itself had been developed as a waiting room with a raised area that had a curved solar wall, and a long upholstered settle. Clients for the demographer could pass their time with a view.

Belatedly, Diment realized that he was being checked in by a receptionist half-hidden in the shrubbery.

First crack out of the box, he thought it was a girl who had swiveled in her office chair to do the honors of the house. Pale gold hair, brown, oval face of a precise classical cast. But the voice came from a speaker well above her head. "Please take a seat. I will ask Mr. Echedemus if he can see you. What is your name?"

Diment parted the foliage and took a closer look. Down to waist level she was all woman. Beyond that threshold, she was a turntable on a single shaft. She had one hand on a call key when he leaned through and grabbed it by the wrist.

Simulation had gone deep. It was warm and textured like regular flesh. Revulsion sharpened the edge on his voice as he said, "Hold fast on that. It won't be necessary. I'm just checking the window seals. Maintenance. Look." He shoved one epaulette forward for a clear scan.

"There was no request for service from this office."

"That's right. But the engineers have a heat loss and we're checking all around. So we start at the top and work down. Which would be a big disappointment in your case. You wouldn't want a draft round your shiny little column, would you?"

Diment made a play of working along the ribs of the solar wall. Outside, it was almost dark and the island was a filigree of colored lights. Over on the mainland, the coast was marked out by the lotus-head beacons, that lit up the long promenade. Smaller lights at sea level were separating out. Small craft racing into the bay. He remembered his own boat. Now it was serving to bring other Wayfarers to the dance macabre.

There was not much time, and it would be a lot easier if he knew positively what he had to do. He went back to the desk.

"What's in the end room? Any likelihood of an open window?"

"The information silo has no glazed surfaces. The files are kept at a constant temperature for preservation."

"What about Nichodemus? Does he have to be at a constant temperature? It's just as well you can't leave your plinth or his mercury would take a surge."

"Mr. *Echedemus* has an observation window."

"I'll check it out."

He was through the wicket and had his hand on the door pull before her memory bank had delivered a riposte.

Opening the door, he said unfairly, "Thank you, I'll go right in."

It was a large room, predominantly gray, shading from off-white walls to the near-black of a three-meter-long executive desk and console. One wall carried a large Op Art abstract of dark and light gray concentric circles, which appeared to spiral in slow movement and carry the mind to some unimaginable deep focus.

The demographer was not easy to pick out. He was two steps off the deck on a broad ledge that ran the length of his observation window and was dressed simply in a Franciscan habit with a gray rope round his middle. The hood was back and framed an austere head with close-cropped gray hair. Movement made him clear as he turned to watch Diment in, with piercing blue eyes deeply set and hooded by thick gray eyebrows.

A deep, resonant voice asked the reasonable question. A demographer's penthouse is his castle. "Who are you? Why were you allowed in here?"

It struck Diment that he might well be the first mainlander to penetrate so far. Wayfarers would be too busy to go searching about and no others recently conditioned to look on an older human used the island. Also, Echedemus would surprise most, but Diment had been recently conditioned to look on an older human face as a natural phenomenon.

"Maintenance crew. Checking for a heat loss. Looks taut as a drum in here. No wandering zephyrs getting up your nighty?"

"What is your number?"

Diment took a moment to invent one and found that he was enjoying himself. Faculties long dormant were being dusted off and stretched. Living dangerously enhanced sensitivity. A timely caution, however, also warned him that too much brinkmanship might put a period to it.

"WR6 oblique 5493 oblique 29."

"I shall have something to say to your Controller. You should not have been sent in here. You are an unusual man. You showed no surprise at seeing me. How long have you worked in this section?"

"Look. Let's not make a big deal out of this. I just want to check your windows. If you say they're okay, I'll get on. There's a lot of ground to cover."

Diment had moved up to the step and ran his hands over the solar wall. It was still warm from the day's heat. But there was more thermal agitation about than it would explain. Echedemus was only a meter away and Diment suddenly realized that he was radiating like a free-standing heater. Not only heat, either. There was a psychokinetic content. Lines of force that were damping out all thought. He was fighting to keep his balance, with gray circles pulsing through his head.

At the same moment of discovery, Echedemus was shaking his wide sleeves free of his hands which were large, sinewy, and full of purpose.

The plummy voice said, "I do not believe you, 5493. We will look more closely at your identity."

One hand grabbed sure and true and closed like a vice on Diment's upper arm.

The contact cleared Diment's head as adrenalin raced round his circuits. Whatever the surface fabric, the hand had a metal core. Echedemus was a very sophisticated android.

With a total concentration of will, Diment dragged the hand gun from his hip pocket and fired point blank into the open mouth and saw the blue eyes mirror fear before they turned up to show white disks. The population adjuster had lost his number-one client.

Carl Borsey reckoned he had missed his vocation. Given a free choice, he would be a cellarman. There was something sympathetic about the amber wood of a barrel that hit a resonant chord in his being. He patted one while he read off the dispatch label on its top—*Regional Farm 7 Euphorics Division. Nut Brown Simulate. W.G.*—followed by a stylized picture of a barley spike.

It was like a short poem to roll off the tongue, and stamped firmly into his memory by seeing the first part on every item in the store.

He was still savoring it when an android with a check list appeared at his side and signaled for a buddy with a neat fork lift truck to roll up and shift it away. Like all the others in the sector, they were enameled olive-drab, which seemed out of character for the chore. For his money, they should have been ruby red and garlanded with leis.

He had done a systematic search job through the bays without finding any point where bulk storage was broken down and some Borgia slipped a powder in the draught. Maybe Diment was on the wrong tack or only the food was fixed. Anything on a big scale would have to be done at this stage. Wayfarers were too thick on the ground for any organizer to check every beaker at the point of issue.

So far, there had been no challenge. All the androids in the sector were manual grade jobs following a program.

Borsey, moved to decision, at a deep level, stepped smartly after his barrel and whipped onto the back step of the dray.

The driver took no notice and drove on to the loading platform of a freight elevator where three others were waiting for a full house. As soon as the incoming weight registered, a portcullis gate dropped behind the trucks and the cage began to rise. There was no conversation. Where human operators would have been rabbiting on about tail or taxes, there was a spell of conservation for fuel cells to stock up urge for the next stint.

Borsey left his truck and went round the other three. Every last crate was marked up with a barley spike, Regional Farm Seven, and the letters W.G.

He had barely completed his tour when the cage rattled to a stop. Before the carrier had finished its rise, the androids were driving out, filling every unforgiving minute with sixty seconds worth of useful labor.

Borsey hopped up again behind his barrel as the convoy moved out. There was not much to see, and he tried to work out what distance he was covering against the ground plan of the island. But there were intersections and changes of direction, all taken without hesitation by the leading driver. All he could fix for sure was that they had covered half a kilometer before the column closed up outside a double-leaf door painted yellow and marked up with *Buttery*.

The leading driver got down jerkily from his footplate and knocked twice like any suppliant at a sect chapel. There was a stage wait to a count of five and both leaves swung open. A tally clerk with a clipboard and an electronic stylus hurried up to check them in.

They were on the inner sector of a huge semicircular bar spread, separated from the distribution area by a screen of narrow yellow spars that ran from floor to ceiling.

Drowning the Wayfarers last thirst was an impressive operation. Nobody was to go short on his favorite tipple if the technocrats could avoid it. A long computer spread chalked up the supply state at every work head along the issue counter, and a task force of fifty general-purpose androids stood ready to plug any gap in the sea wall.

The sheer efficiency of it cured Carl Borsey's thirst. Looked at from this side, it was a calculated insult. Through the gaps in the screen, he could see that the night's work was under way. Still fairly sparse, but dotted along the length, Wayfarers were pouring the products of Regional Farm Seven over their healthy teeth.

An android watching for his number to come up had seen a signal and went into action. The section of spar screen in front of him swiveled briefly on a center pivot, and he was through with a refill as though working a vaudeville vanishing act. There was a short burst of music with a sharp ecstatic beat.

Borsey circulated slowly, watching supplies go forward with precise, efficient movement. There was no tampering with the product in the backroom. If it happened at all it had to be out front under the consumer's eye. He was beginning to think that they were wrong, but to give a full report, he should see the final stage.

He waited for an android to move out and fell in step behind.

Noise bludgeoned him. After the years away from it, he had forgotten the impact of sound on public places. Anything at all could be broadcast under that pervasive carrier wave. In fact, he felt his resolution was being undermined. Why resist it? Go along with the crowd. The majority may be wrong, nevertheless it was always right.

It took a positive effort to remember what he was doing, helped by a musical shriek from a girl in a transparent caftan who pointed a bare arm over the bar and said, "Look at that, then. That one's got an old gorilla after it."

Borsey had time to see that there was a straightforward service. Liquor went from bottle to glass without addition. He also saw that the androids in personal contact with the public were very elegant female simulates, blonde-wigged, faces set in encouraging smiles. Then a number of things happened at once.

One of the barmaids, looking along the girl's pointing arm, recognized a threat and pressed a summoning button for higher judgment. The android he was following made his delivery and wheeled round to retrace his steps. Two sections of the screen whipped open and brought two steel-gray bouncers into the area to the left and right of where he was.

Borwey dropped on one knee and let the serving man fall over him. As his feet left the deck, he straightened up with the main weight of the torso across his shoulders. Then he lifted him at full arm stretch and threw him at the nearest bouncer.

They hit the parquet together like a sack of empty cans and Borsey sidestepped to let the other one plough past and tangle with the heap.

It was all good clean fun and the girl who had taken him for a gorilla was choking over her drink and having to be slapped on her back by an escort.

She had prudently put her tall glass on the bar top and it was still four-fifths full with small bubbles slowly breaking surface. Borsey, exalted by action, took a detour to the bar counter, scooped up the beaker, and tipped the lot down the V of her caftan. Gorilla he might be, but a quick thinker who could join two sticks to get a banana even when under pressure.

Buttons were being pressed all along the line. It was time to go. Borsey whipped through a revolving door and passed another bouncer moving in. The sudden quiet in the back room was like a physical blow. But he reckoned it would not last when the posse got itself sorted. A fork-lift stood ready for the return trip at the buttery door with an android waiting patiently on the seat. It was high time he got himself mechanized.

Borsey took it from the rear, using the back of the seat as a fulcrum and swinging down with all his weight. He did not even look round to see where it fell and had the small motor howling to a crash start. The forks were crashing at the door before the tally man could lift his pencil. Then he was through and bucking down the alley at a hand gallop.

Pamela Harte worked methodically round the kitchen. There was no challenge from the staff even when she broke a test sample from a cornucopia modeled in marzipan simulate and stuffed with exotic truffles.

She started a second tour at the point where raw materials were issued from dispenser chutes. This large scale operation for processing biological fuel for the human crop was depressing when you got right down to it. Where did they part company with the androids anyway?

She remembered her pre-Wayfarer life. Stints at the android assembly plant, where she was employed as a reader putting vocabulary lists into their memory banks. Somewhere about there would be androids with *her* voice, using a word collection not much smaller than her own. In some ways their self-energizing power packs were more efficient than her own temperamental metabolism. Who was to say what they were thinking as they went about their business? Maybe they were the heirs to progress and simple organic evolution had passed its peak.

Intellect could accept it as a reasonable proposition, but intuition rejected it. There was more to a human being than a collection of behavioristic phenomena. She wished she had done more thinking in the past. Why hadn't she, then? There had to be something in what Roger Diment said. They had been got at and kidded along as consumers without a critical thought.

The first, long preparation spread closed off the wall where the delivery chutes brought in the staples, and there was no visible way through. She stopped opposite a batch of chicken carcasses ready for the spit and was reminded of the conveyer in the basement. With heroic resolution, she vaulted over the counter and touched down in front of an android in a tall chef's hat who had picked that time to appear from between two supply chutes.

At the same instant an alarm bleep sounded from somewhere above her head. Although there had been no visible reaction to her presence on the set, there must have been an overall monitor system that had been watching and looking for any move that might disrupt the system.

The chef had a plain ovoid head with a single glowing visual receptor in the center of its notional forehead. Pamela Harte had a wild idea that it was transmitting her picture to some point farther off. If she could stop it, she would be invisible.

Spaced along the rear of the counter were open plastic bins for disposal of rejects. With a neat, smooth action she grabbed up the nearest, which was half full of giblets, and upended it at full arm stretch over his head.

It settled with a thud onto his shoulders. Pamela Harte had a sudden thought that the single bright eye would be peering in darkness through a mass of entrails and felt her throat contract with nausea. But it was effective. He stood stock still, out of program, and she ducked past his waving arms into the space between the machines.

Out back was the bulk break down area. Nothing there to show any sign of tampering with the incoming food. Sacks and packing cases were stacked for return. All bore the same legend. There was a barley spike symbol and *Regional Farm Seven. Euphorics Division. W.G.*

The alarm bleep was sounding even here and androids were halting in their labor to take special instruction. Time to get out and rejoin Diment like a faithful gleaner with her barley spike.

She ran the length of the bay, weaving past general purpose androids who had no skill outside their limited manual duties. It was a dead end. There was no way out. On the way back, she saw that every entry from the main kitchen had an android posted to close off any return that way.

The androids in the bay had shuffled round until they were shoulder to shoulder and closing in a narrowing arc to pen her against a solid wall.

God, they were stupid to think they could do anything against such a system. This was the end. A second trip on the conveyer with no reawakening. She gave way slowly step by step with the circle contracting. She felt the smooth wall at her back.

Tears pricked her eyes. But it was not for herself that she was crying. She was glad of that. It was for the whole stupid mess that her race had gotten itself into.

They were not two meters off, a solid wall of metal, hands stretching out. At least she would not scream. Even when the probing fingers touched, she would not scream.

CHAPTER FIVE

Roger Diment heard the voice from the console as a background noise, but was not tuned in to read its message. He was totally occupied with Echedemus who had slumped dramatically over the steps to his observation platform like any martyred senator.

There was a flow of blood from his open mouth and Diment, with a sample on his index finger, was baffled by it. Not a doubt, it was human blood.

Under the off-white robe, Echedemus was finely made. Every joint an engineer's rave in articulation, sheathed in the most accurate skin simulate that technology could devise, though on the feminine side for a male model.

But for all that, he was, or had been—if that was the way to look at it—no more than a mechanical marvel. What was the point of blood? That was carrying the human similarity too far for no purpose.

The voice from the console notched itself up on the decibel scale and went into a third repeat. It was the stool-bound receptionist trying to raise her employer.

74

"Mr. Echedemus. I have a priority call for you. Will you take it, please?"

Diment had stripped off the robe and had it over his arm. He struggled into it on the way to the desk and pulled the hood closely round his face. Flipping switches on the panel, he first brought up the operator's face and said curtly, "Go ahead."

While he waited for the connection, he thought a man could easily get excited about that one, just seeing her over a video, and yet she petered out in a swivel shaft. There was a philosophical point there somewhere, but this was no time to hound it to its hole. The screen blanked and glowed again with another face.

He had not switched himself to transmit and there was an irritable query. "Are you there Echedemus? What's the delay?"

Diment had gotten himself into the executive seat and sat well back, selecting focus three, which brought him in as a small inset with a fair spread of neutral office wall as a backdrop. The caller, anxious to push his business, accepted it as adequate for social comfort and got down to cases without preamble.

"An unusual situation has developed. Two alarms in the reception area. Intruders have been active in the food preparation center and in a euphorics dispensary."

"So?"

"I am surprised you have no other comment. It cannot be coincidence. It must be a deliberate attempt to gather information. However, we shall soon know. One of them, a female, has been taken. She could be in the Wayfarer age group, but the other one according to report is considerably older.

That is very interesting. I want you to join me at once. You can assist in the interrogation."

"Of course. Where are you?"

"In the operations room, where else? The majority of the crop is already in. It is important that we clear this matter as quickly as possible. This may well be the lead we were waiting for. I shall expect you in three minutes."

The screen blanked and Diment used ten seconds in a quick scan round the office. Three minutes put the operations room somewhere close in the tower block; but he could spend half an hour checking every level. There was no diagram to be seen.

There was, however, a closet hardly more than a deep cupboard, fitted with racks holding the demographer's personal files of microtape. He lugged the body in by its heels and stood it up with one hand realistically reaching for a shelf.

The receptionist swiveled slowly to watch him out of the office. As he reached the wicket gate she said, "Where can I call you, sir?"

"Operations."

She slid open a panel on her desk top and revealed a schematic layout. Drawing a stylus out of a retaining socket, she marked in a small upper-case E on the thirteenth level.

Leaning over and reading upside down, Diment checked off the printed names in the spaces left and right. One said *Controller Magnes,* the other *Personnel Adviser, Miss Y. Raidney.* It was enough for a navigational fix.

Concentrating on it, he had let the cowl fall away from his face and he met the receptionist's eye, which was all accusation and wild surmise. She even had an index finger pointing at his chest like a good citizen about to indict an aristo at the city gate.

Diment, whose conscience was still tender, said irritably, "Don't do that," and followed up by taking the denunciatory digit and bending it at right angles to the back of the elegant hand. Where a human operator would have pushed a cry from the heart, the android was only concerned to get a report in the right channels. Her other hand scurried along the keyboard for an all services call.

Diment, a living proof that the human brain still had the edge on a computerized system, beat it by a centimeter and knocked off the master key that left the network dead. It also froze the operator in a still. Wig awry, finger up, eyes glazed with effort, she was a surrealist study.

Given time, the reawakened man could have found a caption, but he remembered Pamela Harte and the set of her shoulders as she walked out of the cage. With the hand gun hidden in a hanging sleeve, he ran for the elevator and shoved in the selector for level thirteen.

Pamela Harte would not have believed that she could prefer the hoi polloi of the kitchen service to anybody at all, but experience, that unflagging teacher, was working at it. The four robed figures in the operations room had the air of inquisitors who would be prepared to watch her slowly dismembered until they got at the truth. If there had been an iron maiden on the set, she would have been in it with one of them turning the screw. Probably the female at that.

Nobody had touched her yet. She had been clipped at wrists and ankles, feet astride, arms outstretched, to a plain bulkhead opposite a long display panel, which was divided into many half-meter squares, each showing a picture of a different part of the complex.

Android operators, sitting in a long line at a continuous desk top below the screen, had not looked up when she was brought in and made no effort to turn round to see what was happening. She realized that she was right at the center of the local organization. She also guessed that nobody would allow her to leave it, with or without information.

The woman, with her cowl off and a button-through variant robe open to show a close-fitting trifle of bronze mesh, made her feel clumsy and inadequate. From her auburn hair, which swung elastically as she moved, to her small feet in gold strap sandals, she was flawless. Only her voice had no warmth. It was a cool, lightweight job, on the high side. It was currently saying, "We should not wait any longer for Echedemus, Controller; she will soon see the wisdom of telling what we want to know. I will make her speak."

Tallest of the three men, a lanky egghead with iron-gray hair, who was standing behind the workers, turned round and put himself a meter from the wall flower. He looked at Pamela, but answered his colleague. "Your zeal does you every credit, Miss Raidney. But interrogation proceeds from the known to the unknown. The demographer will identify her and turn up her file. Then we shall have a starting point. I am concerned with information. When I have that, you may do with her as you please."

There was no change of expression on the Raidney face, which was set in a permanent smile stemming from justifiable self-regard; but a very red tongue appeared briefly and touched the center of her upper lip.

Pamela Harte shivered in spite of the room's sub-tropical heat. The girl's age could be anywhere from twenty on, but the Controller was much older. Near-er Bedall's age. The implications of that took her mind off herself.

His eyes were very pale green with pinpoint pupils, watching her with an unblinking stare. He said, "You are thinking about age. You are wondering how and why we have passed the Wayfarer stage. But you are not as surprised as might be expected. You have seen others who have avoided that necessary stop. You have recently made great strides in intel-lectual growth. You have passed the immature stage, when you and your immediate wants were the only motivating forces. Given time, you would mature into an interesting person. But time, unfortunately, is what you do not have."

Nobody likes to be an open book. Pamela Harte said, "If you know so much, why bother to ask? Go and play with your electronic organ."

The personnel adviser had moved up and reck-oned that the top hand needed her special skill. She leaned forward and jabbed twice, palm down, fingers extended, as though testing a lay figure for compressive stress.

It was casually done, but the payoff was out of all proportion to the simple act. Pamela Harte strained against her clips in an arc of agony and had screamed once before she could control her mouth.

Diment, coming through the hatch, had only backs to look at as the four inquisitors waited for the spasm to pass. The scene etched itself on his retina; watchful stillness and human despair. What-ever vague plan had been forming to play along as Echedemus in a search for information was drowned

out in a red tide. He shot twice at the two nearer
figures as though picking off targets on a range.
They were still deciding which way to fall when he
said, "Whoever put her in there, get her out."

Magnes was fishing for something in a deep pocket of his robe and Pamela, still struggling for a
pain-free breath, gasped out, "Watch his hand."

Hidden from Diment, it was free of the hanging
cuff holding a small compact blaster with a bulbous
barrel.

Pamela was a penumbra round the target, at risk
from any shot missing by a millimeter. Diment
threw every gram of urge into a sprint start and
was up close before the Controller could half turn.
He had a neck lock on and one hand clamped on
the wrist with the gun and asked a question in a
voice that surprised Pamela Harte.

Pain had drained away to two centers of dull
ache, leaving her sensitive to every nuance in the
situation. Diment sounded as though he could be
the sadist of all time, and she reckoned she had been
lucky not to cross him in their brief relationship.

"Think fast, Magnes. Find one good reason why
I shouldn't break your lousy head off its stalk."

Answer came from the female partner, who had
used her portion of time to slip out of her robe and
stood revealed in her crotch-length mesh like a
bronze Venus stepping from a scallop shell. A generous plunge in the neckline carried to the navel,
showed a dazzling triangle of white skin with delicate
circular relief to intrigue any human geographer.
"You are too hasty. Look at me. Do you think I
would be a party to anything that was wrong? This
girl has damaged valuable androids. We have to
find out why she was acting that way. Be reasonable."

Tone had deepened by a key. Now she sounded

all womanly concern and her beauty hit Diment like a velvet cosh. Logic missed a link. He did not equate her with Echedemus. She had to be for real.

Pamela Harte said bitterly, "She's the worst of the lot. Don't listen to her."

Magnes, sensing a slackening of purpose, said, "Let us be intelligent about this. I will release the girl, then we will discuss the situation together." At the same time, he tried to twist his right hand out of Diment's grip.

It was a premature move and triggered Diment at an instinctive level. Confusing the situation might well be; but it was clear enough that an armed man should not be given freedom of action. He shoved his left knee into the Controller's back and heaved smartly at the neck in the crook of his left arm.

There was a definitive click and he was holding a dead weight. He let the body find its own level on the deck and stepped clear.

Miss Raidney was halfway to the console, moving well with a neatly undulating can. He said almost apologetically, "Hold it there, Ginger, one more step and I'll blast a hole through that sexy dress. Come over here and be a help."

Accustomed to giving advice, she had no difficulty in balancing the merits and demerits. She stopped in mid-stride and swung round ready to oblige a polite asker.

Familiarity had blunted some of the impact, but Diment watched her cross to Pamela's piece of wall as though he had never seen anything quite like it. Which was true enough.

Andromeda herself, still chained to her rock, reckoned she was getting a poor deal. She said, "For godsake, take that ridiculous simper off your face, Roger Diment, and get me out of here."

"You heard the lady."

Miss Raidney realized that, in spite of superficial progress, she would get nowhere on the main count at this stage and flipped a recessed switch. The gyves opened and Pamela Harte stepped free, rubbing her wrists. She said, "Let's get the hell out of here. But first I have a score to settle with this smooth monkey."

She dropped on one knee beside Magnes and pried the blaster from his fingers.

Unused to the violent life, she was some seconds sorting out the mechanism and Diment, given a cooling period, saw it as cold-blooded murder.

He had time to deflect the aim and a thin searing beam, brilliant as a magnesium flare, missed the Personnel Adviser by a hand's breadth and scorched a charred line in the paneling.

The Raidney smile, momentarily switched off, was back again with hardly a break. She said, "That was wise. Killing solves nothing. Tell me what you are doing here. Perhaps I can help you."

Diment, impressed by the blaster, took it from Pamela's suddenly limp hands and substituted it for the hand gun. As a specialist, he appreciated its balance and the functional shaping. There was nothing like it on the firing ranges. It was yet another proof that they were technically outclassed by whoever was running the higher organization.

"You might just do that. For a start you can say who you are and what you do here. I don't recall ever seeing these robed characters about in the city."

"I'll be frank with you."

"That's nice."

"Truly. You wouldn't see us. There are only twenty-one Organizers at present in this city. We are here for a period to superintend the Wayfarer . . . arrangement." The pause before the word was small, but measurable. She had been about to use another and made a quick switch. But she went on without a change in the friend-winning smile. "After a three-year tour of duty, we are relieved. Seven change each year for continuity reasons, as you will appreciate."

Diment was doing a rapid sum. With Echedemus lodged in his closet, three down on the parquet, and the Personnel Adviser present in the fair flesh, it left sixteen going about their master's business. Not too far away either. He couldn't always win. Even now, very now, others could be on the way to chat up Magnes in the operations room.

To Pamela Harte he said, "Have a look at that one. See if he's carrying one of these handy blasters." He went to the nearest and rolled him over. Sure enough, in the deep right-hand pocket of his robe was another.

Pamela Harte, nerves crawling with distaste, pulled out a third. Quicker off the mark this time to see how it worked, she had the catch thumbed down and was all set to carry through her unfinished business, when Diment said, "Hold it, you little spitfire. Where's your magnanimity?"

Wherever it was, it was well under control. Memory had not played false. She knew for a truth that the Raidney would be well shuffled off and her expression was an amalgam of desperate resolve and horror at the thing to be done.

But it was all wasted. Different their intentions might be, but they were both looking in vain. In the few seconds out of direct view, she had worked her personal variant of the Indian Rope Trick and had vacated her slot in space. Only the empty robe was a mute proof that she had existed at all.

Diment said, "Her office is next door, she must have slipped through. Look for a sliding panel."

"We should go. She'll be on the blower calling for help."

It was true, but he was suddenly held by another development. The multiscreen spread was showing a key stage in the Wayfarer saga. Every last one had the same kind of picture. Some at the banquet tables, some on the dance floors, singly or in pairs, frozen in every act that caprice or passion could conjure with, the Wayfarers were still as waxworks. The only movement was from androids going impassively through the Saturnalia, checking identity bracelets, loading the chosen on their hospital trolleys, and carting them off for their long journey to oblivion.

Pamela Harte, shocked out of her vendetta, dropped the blaster and put both hands to her cheeks. She said unsteadily, "I'm ashamed. We must have looked like that. I can't even remember who I was with. What's the point, Roger? We're not worth saving. It would have been better not to know."

"They're not themselves. We were not ourselves. Like somnambulists."

"But it's there in the mind or it wouldn't come out. What is a human being after all?"

"The only begetter of this system. Who invented the androids? Somewhere along the line there's been a wrong turn into a cul-de-sac."

The small click of a released catch made a period. Diment scooped up the fallen blaster and had one in either hand to range around the room. But no panel slid clear. The opposition had no wish to shoot it out.

He said, "On your way Pamela, out into the corridor. As of now we have a duty to stay in one piece. Maybe the answer will be made plain."

At the door he turned for another look. The three Organizers were unmoved, nothing more to do there. But he could put the computer out of action for a spell. A long burst of white flame seared along the spread and panels imploded in succession. Tongues of flame and black smoke jetted out. The operators went slack like puppets with broken strings, slumping over the desk top. Fault indicators came out in a red rash, went into overload, and gave up.

Diment was out in the corridor and did not see the three Organizers who followed Miss Raidney into the operations room. One of them, who could have been Magnes's younger brother, said, "Magnes had only himself to blame. I have been saying ever since I arrived here that there should be a full-scale investigation. Now it will be done. Miss Raidney, send in a report to Urania City on the closed link, of course. Rate it orange priority and ask for a contingent of the special force to be sent before morning. This will be settled once and for all."

"Certainly, Subcontroller Madigan."

"Controller, as of now. When you have done that come into my office."

"Certainly, Controller. What about the man and the woman?"

"They will not get far. All the island is on alert. Pollitt has them monitored. Be patient. Your special skills will have their use later."

To Diment's jaundiced eye androids appeared to be growing by spontaneous creation out of every crevice. He was tired of picking them off. Against the blasters they had no chance. But there were so many. In the end, numbers alone would do it. Charges would run out and they would be overwhelmed.

He also knew for a truth that somebody had them in vision all the way. Somewhere in the heap an operator was marshaling these forces and coldly sending them to be chopped down as a delaying tactic.

The unarmed general-purpose androids were pathetic; like sending peasants against a man in armor. But the black security guards, though thin on the ground, were a different proposition. Each time it was a duel that he only just won. A little slackening of concentration, a small break in the teamwork pattern that had them halving the scene to watch both fronts, and it would be all over.

For a brief space, they were in a no-man's land, between floors on the spiral service stairs, Pamela Harte going first with her dark ringlet swaying emotionally across the nape of her neck. Confused by the twist, she was in a limbo, dropping down a bottomless well. Somewhere in her head a ticker tape started up and she read off message. "Give yourself up. Stop running. You cannot fight the whole world. This is the way it is. Give up. Stop running."

She missed a step and Diment's arm round her chest kept her from taking a header down the flight.

They stopped in dynamic balance, half leaned against the wall. Diment felt the firm tumescence of her breasts against his forearm and tried to turn her round. But she had both hands flat on the curved bulkhead and would not move.

He dropped down to the same level, crowded against her in the narrow space, and put his lips against her right ear. She could feel him lining her back like a warm, animated rug.

"What is it, Pamela?"

The incoming signal was fainter, she could hardly see the printing on the tape. But it was still there as a vague compulsion. She said dully, "It's no use. We can't go on. We have to give up."

"Who says so?"

"I keep getting it loud and clear in my head."

Unexpectedly, he said, "So do I. Take no notice. That's what they want. We can't stop now."

Using a wrestler's ploy he relaxed his grip as though he was moving away and she dropped her hands from the wall. In a flash he had her twisted from her holdfast and facing him. There was not a lot of time for a staff morale exercise, but he managed to give the impression that there was plenty for grooming talk.

"What's a beautiful girl like you doing with a pessimistic outlook?"

Before she could present a detailed manifest with a whole raft of good evidence marshaled under alphabetical sections, he bent his head and effectively shut her mouth. Lips were full, soft, and slightly salt, remaining closed for a count of five, then opening slowly as her hands locked behind his head.

The ticker tape stopped and faded out. Diment knew it was so and said, "There you are. It's easy. That's all we have to do to beat this mind bending bit. Take this prophylactic action a little farther and we'd be transmitting a counterblast. Eros is life. Love equals mc^2. Stay close and just lift your right hand when you want a booster shot."

From the floor below came a muted rattle of shots.

Pamela Harte said, "Carl. Let's go," and was down three steps before he had moved.

Every succeeding turn made it clear. Diment recognized pistol fire. Androids then, rather than Organizers with their refined blasters.

One more turn and they stood together on a small square landing with a green painted sliding door which marked a floor level. There was a surge of sound coming up from the right. Diment eased it open a crack and looked out.

Coming along like a runaway and lurching left and right to defy all laws of stability, a fork lift truck was beating up the alley with Carl Borsey bent double to reduce target area. Fifty meters behind him, four black androids were pounding along.

Diment slid the door full open and yelled "Carl" as the truck thundered past. Left of the door, perhaps thirty meters off, another contingent of security guards was drawn up shoulder to shoulder, blocking the whole corridor width.

Diment dived full length into the open with a blaster in either hand and sprayed two incandescent beams the way Borsey had come.

The four guards gathered a nimbus of blue flame like St. Elmo's fire. They came on three more steps and then stopped as the instant furnace heat ran their circuitry into a mash.

At his back Diment heard the crash and whipped round in time to see the charioteer dive from the truck as it hit.

One android was still on his feet and the hornet wow of slugs came chest high down the passage. Diment made a marksman's job of it and sent a beam to hit precisely in the center of the ovoid casque, like an unfolding flower of brilliant light.

There was a lull. Except for one android beating

aimlessly about in the heap with its directional gear running wild. Pamela Harte ran to Borsey, who was swearing in a monotone and trying to get to his feet.

"It's this goddamned leg. I fell right on it." He was speaking through clenched teeth, his face gray with pain.

Between them they got him standing, holding on, arms round their shoulders.

Pamela Harte said, "Hold on, Carl. You'll make it. You're a natural for a hospital scene. We'll get you the best looking nurse in the outfit to feed you little bowls of nourishing soup and that."

The stairs were out for a five-leg trio. Diment did a rapid reappraisal of the situation. He had been aiming for the conveyer tunnel; but in any case that would have been a highly suspect route. For one, they would easily seal off either end and for another, it would put the finger definitely on the museum complex. This clinched it. They had to go outside and make it overland.

They were at the cellar level, beside a different elevator trunk from the one they had used to go up; two floors below ground. They had been seen to be making for the basement. Maybe a change of direction would catch the opposition on the wrong tin foot.

He signaled for a cage and they waited for it to come, blasters trained on the grille, more than half sure it would be full of security gribbles. But when it moved soundlessly to a stop it was empty.

Borsey tried to help by swinging his good leg, but the movement made him break out in a cold sweat and they lifted him the last meter.

Diment, remembering axioms of first aid, said, "Look. We have to immobilize you. Use the good leg as a splint and strap the other one to it. God knows what damage you'll be doing."

There was room to lie him diagonally across the floor and Pamela Harte, in the best traditions of the Crimea, shrugged out of her coveralls, started a break with her teeth, and began to tear off useful strips.

Borsey said, "I see what you mean. Every situation has its recompense," and patted the worker's taut black briefs.

Nightingale-Harte said, "That's enough of that or I'll jump on your fracture."

The cage stopped. As the door sliced away, Diment was out on the landing and fetched up with his back to the facing wall, searching for a target. But the space was empty, drab and neglected, with a stack of baled trash half filling the area. There was a sweet smell of decay, an unused corner of the complex.

Beside the dump there was a door with a round glass port high up. It was showing a star map. Another door, facing it, led back into the ground floor of the tower block. Both were locked. Rhythmic thumps from somewhere close told that the directing genius had switched a task force to flush them out.

Diment shot through the lock of the outer door, kicked it open, and rejoined Pamela Harte. They gripped wrists and heaved Borsey off the deck between them so that he was sitting up with his legs stuck straight out.

They were ten meters off, on soft ground between two rhododendron shrubs when they heard the inner door fall with a percussive smack and a spotlight from somewhere high up in the building began to sweep around trying to pick them up.

Borsey was thumping Diment's back with a balled fist. "Stop right here. Put me down, I tell you. Pamela, make the stupid sod listen to sense."

They were at the head of a short ramp that led to the long mole that curved out from the island in a quarter circle. Four meters wide, it had a stepped parapet on the sea side and made a sheltered anchorage for small craft and a quay for deeper draught freight tenders. Hurrying lights, converging from every point on land, marked the progress of the dragnet. It was unbelievable that they had gotten so far.

For the last two hundred meters Diment had carried the load himself in a fireman's lift and was more tired than he would have believed possible and still able to take a forward step.

He said thickly, "Not far now, Carl. We'll do it."

"Not like this you won't. As soon as those zombies get to hard ground, they'll come on at a run. You've got to find a boat and get it started. This is my choice. Put me down."

Diment stopped to think it through. Pamela trailing four meters called urgently, "They've reached the road."

Borsey had one of the blasters and shoved it in Diment's ear. "Drop me or I swear to god I'll blast your fool head off."

The leading androids had picked up their silhouettes against the night sky and began to fire.

Diment said wearily, "All right Carl, you win."

"I want the hand gun. You can never be sure when this fancy gadget will pack up."

Pamela Harte said, "We can't leave you. If we do that we're no better than they are."

"You can and you will. The future lies with you. I don't mind. Remember that. I don't mind. It's that tide bit. There'll never be a better time for me. Don't deny me that."

A ricochet from the stone parapet whined out over the bay. Diment grabbed her hand and they ran, bent low.

Behind them there was a flare and then another. Following the curve of the mole, they could look back.

Borsey was braced against the sea wall covering the apron. Until he was hit or his charges ran out, no android could pass.

Diment found what he was looking for. She was lying twenty meters off, riding to a mooring buoy, a pale blur on the wine dark sea.

Without a check he dived from the mole, a shock therapy that galvanized him into fresh life. He was under the square transom grabbing for the chain before he thought that he had not asked whether Pamela could swim. But she was nowhere in sight and he set himself to climb aboard feeling dead weight on his aching arms.

Then he was tearing a canvas cover from the cockpit lit by a continuous flare of light from the land which confirmed the name of the craft, *Sea Urchin,* in Gothic script on the cabin bulkhead.

The motor fired and he lay flat along the deck to see Pamela Harte's sleek black head not a meter off. Heels hooked in the coaming, he stretched down and heaved her aboard, cold skin of her midriff against his face.

He knocked free the shackle and gunned for full ahead making a tight creaming turn for the shore.

Pamela Harte, crouched at the bow, sobbed, "It's too late. They've got to him."

In the last flare of the blaster, they saw the

apron packed with androids running now for the mole.

The flare burned out. There was a single pistol shot.

Diment spun the wheel and raced for the channel to the open sea.

CHAPTER SIX

Pamela Harte at the prow felt the switch from the harbor to the open sea as a final step in dissociation.

Sea Urchin slapped into a long swell and lifted her foot as Diment spun the throttle for full power. A creaming bow wave ran off into the dark. An astringent wind tightened her salty skin. The past was finally dead, absolved in some special way by Carl Borsey's personal sacrifice.

There would be a time to think about that and remember it; but now they were outside the system and could see it whole. Whatever it cost they had to rouse their kind from the complacency that had grown up like a thickset hedge. It was a complete program, if low on detail. She felt illuminated by it; also, grateful to the man at the wheel who had given her this second run at the data.

She stood up impulsively and balance-walked over the canting deck to the cockpit. Diment reached up with a free hand and gathered her in.

On their small hurrying platform, they could have been anywhere dark and sprayswept, consciousness reduced to a pinpoint in an endless sea. But it was enough; a seed to grow from.

Hands flat on his chest, she had her wet hair against his chin, content not to see, accepting whatever was to come.

Sea Urchin drummed on. Diment woke to the physical fact that he was holding a cold nude. He said gently, "You'll get frostbite in your extremities. Nip below and see what the cabin has to offer."

"Don't you like me the way I am?"

"Because I like you the way you are I want to preserve you in good working order for a more propitious time."

"That sounds like a stall."

"One of the sound principles of the seafaring life is that the crew never argues. It says 'Aye, aye Sir' and knuckles its forelock."

"I don't think I have one."

"I am not a harsh man. Any reasonable substitute will be A-Okay."

"I'll think of something."

Cold lips briefly brushed the side of his jaw. Then she was ducking under the coaming into the narrow cabin. A roof light went on and their small world was extended by five meters with a long plexiglass inset in the deckhead glowing like a pointing finger.

Her voice filtered back against the rush of water and the hiss of the propulsion jets. "She's provisioned for a trip. All kinds of tinned food. Coffee. Sweaters. With *Sea Urchin*. All very nautical. No peaked caps, though. Slacks. And sneakers. I'll kit out and take over for a spell, then you can change."

She did better than that. When she finally reappeared on deck in a tomato red jersey with the craft's name in pleasant high relief, she was carrying a steaming mug of ship's cocoa in either hand.

In the aftermath of action, Diment was feeling cold. He said, "Well done, Jim lad. One day I'll let you play with my parrot."

"I can't wait."

They drank the scalding hot brew in companionable silence.

Lights from high-rise apartments in the city were closer, picked out now as discrete objects, apparently hanging above the horizon with the low-lying land still hidden.

Reluctant to break the bond, but knowing that action and decision were rushing in from ahead, Diment said, "Steady as you go. Watch for outlying banks. There's been shoaling all along this coast. I reckon it's okay for another five minutes, then drop to half speed and be ready to go about."

"Aye, aye Sir."

"You're learning fast. I'll be right back."

Left to herself, Pamela Harte checked round the console. A bank of piano keys beside the wheel took her eye and she pressed them in turn.

The first lit a hidden searchlight in the bow and a long beam arrowed out over the sea. On the second there was no immediate joy, then a dark shadow engulfed her from the stern and her startled "Eek" brought Diment head and shoulders out of the hatch.

"What is it?"

"Did you know we had a convertible? There's a rain hood that comes up at a touch."

"Keep your eye on the course. Don't mess about."

Number three dropped open a small square panel and revealed a palm-sized radio with button tuning. She pressed for Barnston City and got the tail end of the signal bleeps for 0100 hours. The first newscast of the new day was coming up for all those still out and about. It was the verbal backing of the actualizer program. More sophisticated gear would have the reader standing there in 3-D to say his piece and selected pictures to prove he told no lie.

The voice itself was enough to point up the seriousness of the message. Clearly the man was showing faithful models of the people he described.

She said urgently, "Roger. Be quick. They're on to us."

Diment stood with one arm round her shoulders and they heard. "The City Council has taken the unusual step of declaring the man and the woman outfarers. This is a technical description which means they are outside the ordinary run of the legal code. They are not entitled to legal representation; they have no rights of any kind. No action would be taken against any citizen who killed or injured them. The Actualities news team has been researching for a precedent and had to go back seventy-five years in the record to find a parallel. Later in the bulletin, you will have a reconstruction of that famous case. As of now, take another look at this latterday Bonnie and Clyde. The man, Roger Diment. Eighty kilograms. Two meters. Fair. Blue eyes. Athletic build. Weaponry expert. The woman, Pamela Harte, fifty point five kilograms, one point six meters, nine fourteen, six ten, nine fourteen. Dark brown hair, hazel eyes. Android programming operative."

There was a pause for the viewing public to take an eyeful. Lacking a picture, the two criminal types looked at each other in the mellow light of the binnacle.

Diment said, "Nine fourteen, six ten, nine fourteen gives no proper indication at all of the satisfactory way you fill out that sweater. Statistics may not lie, but what they conceal is vital."

"You don't have to jolly me along. I can understand. With that newscast going out twenty-four times a day, we'll be recognized everywhere. It's a death warrant."

"Not necessarily. Back in the museum, they can do a lot with costume and make up."

"How do we get there?"

It was a good question and hung about unanswered.

Diment said, "For that matter, it wouldn't be hard for them to have this boat on a scan. All that cock on the newscast is to leave no stone unturned. There'll be a highly mobile party at the marina ready to run along the coast when it's clear where we must land."

"So it's hopeless."

"Not quite. Switch the headlight on."

"Then they'll pick us up for sure. Good thinking."

"Even an android will not search for what he has already found."

"What is a simple girl to make of that sententious bit?"

"I like you all bare and wet. You're going for another swim."

"I don't like you, going on in this riddling vein. Pretend I don't know what you're on about and explain it straight."

"About half a kilometer off shore, we turn and run parallel, as though looking for a place to land. Then I spike the wheel and we slip over the side. *Sea Urchin* goes it alone with the gribbles jogging along the esplanade waving their riot sticks. We walk ashore without let or hindrance."

"Pretending it's all just a social dip and that we're really two other people."

"I saw life jackets in the locker and storage bags. Shove the clothes in a cover and they're dry to put on. Okay?"

"If you say so."

The moment came sooner than Pamela Harte expected. On the crest of a swell, the shore was suddenly all too near—a long white line where the seas broke, backed by the pale blur of the long esplanade and its rows of bright amber standard beacons. Over left, the landlocked marina was sewn with the riding lights of anchored craft. Over right, the land curved out to a point five or six kilometers off.

Sea Urchin would hit right at the land tip.

Diment jammed the wheel and watched for a count of ten. She was holding course and steady as a rock. She would make some leeway; but not enough to matter in the distance. Pamela was on the rail ready to go. Eyes and teeth shining in the light. He shut the power by a quarter and said, "Okay. Let's go."

At sea level, they lost sight of the shore. The *Marie Celeste* beat away with its beam probing out into the sea and they were alone with the ghosts of all mariners left by a foundering ship. Diment was thinking back through his argument. There was no flaw in it, except one. The reality of the cold impact with the sea itself had been left out. Theory was right on the button, practice could prove it false. It was too far and too cold. He set himself to endure, swimming alongside Pamela Harte, whose white buttocks broke from the dark surface in two pale ovals, a witch in a pool in an endless cave.

It had been well under the hour, but it could have been any length of time in days. Diment was going on because he was programmed to go on, but there was no sense or feeling in it. When his feet dragged on a sand bar, he still swam until the life jacket under his chest grounded on the slope of the beach and he lay like a half-tide rock. Fastened by a tether to the jacket straps, Pamela Harte drifted in, still going through the motions of a weary crawl, and nudged soggily at his side.

Diment felt the prod, got himself on hands and knees, and crawled forward, floundering through a deeper pool and then to the line of sea wrack.

The low tide smell cleared his head. They were ashore.

Any low-grade android could have led him in and claimed a bonus of perfumed oil. But there was none to see him stand up, struggle painfully up the shingle beach, hauling Pamela Harte on the line like a bemused fish, and settle again in fine soft sand with his back to the sea wall.

Looking out to sea, his eyes were automatically taken by the only moving object in vision. A bright pointer was moving slowly to the extreme tip of the bay. Memory came in with a rush. *Sea Urchin* was within minutes of making a landfall.

Diment tore clumsily at the seals on the fetch bag and tipped the gear onto the sand. Then he was rousing Pamela Harte out of comfortable torpor and shoving a towel into her unwilling hands. Protesting to the last, she was ready to go on as the light stopped moving. *Sea Urchin* had run aground.

They crossed the broad esplanade at a run, vaulted a low wall, and were in shadow again in a fifty-meter belt of ornamental gardens. Further in was the service road that ringed the coast. Beyond that a narrow strip of gardens and parking bays backed by all night bars, fun places, and all the paraphernalia of joy.

There was still some action there and a gusty land breeze brought snatches of music; computerized melody, calculated to the last crotchet to jerk nostalgia out of a fossil log.

They fetched up outside a long plate-glass spread, the open end of a womb-like cave with deep red drapes and minimum lighting. Service was still being given to a scatter of determined revelers in alcoves off the main hall. In the center of the floor a multifaceted jukebox glowed with shifting drifts of intense color. Above it, apparently suspended by a trick of levitation, a nude in a glass box was dancing to the beat with elaborate contortion. The legend etched in the glass named the place "The One-Handed Clap."

Purified in the fire of experience, Pamela Harte said censoriously, "Why don't they grow up? Fiddling while Rome burns, to coin a phrase. Those damned androids must be laughing in their tin guts."

True or false, the ministrants to the wake were gliding about with fixed encouraging smiles. No aching feet or memory of a waiting bed brought incivility to the service.

Diment handed over one of the blasters. "Get along to the powder room. Grab somebody your size and change clothes. Make for this end alcove. If there's any trouble, don't wait for me, get out. Hide away somewhere and make for the museum at opening time. Good luck."

Used to clients from the Marina, there was no comment as they pushed open the inner door from a small lobby like a pressure lock to insulate the cave from the world of sea and air.

Inside, there was less doubt why people stayed on; tropical heat, pervasive rhythm that blanked the mind, a diffusion of exaltolides that gave the air a tangible impact like breathing thin syrup. It was only remarkable that anybody had any will left to leave again.

Even the washroom had the music piped in and screens on every wall, so that customers missed no wriggle in the dancer's repertoire. Diment took a quick shower to sluice off sand and salt and waited for his victim.

When the man came with a slow somnambulist's step, eyes wide and unfocused, almost all pupil, it was too easy to be true.

He was almost Diment's height, but with a close-shaven head so that a uniform cap of short fair bristle covered his skull. He was wearing red slacks, a blue-green tunic heavily frogged with yellow brocade, and had picked up a fresh lei from the stand outside.

Diment stepped behind him and chopped scientifically into the side of his neck, crushing a flower. Then he left him leaned back realistically in a loo, watching a miniature screen with unseeing eyes, locked the door from the inside, and climbed out all fixed for the bacchanals.

The identity bracelet said he was now Horace Johnson, serial BC/4005/37, a Graphics Consultant domiciled in residential block 29. There was a room key, a combination hatch and activator key for shuttle number zero-zero-eight, and a pad of credit slips in the only pocket in the tunic. And from what had been torn off, it looked as though Horace was a big spender in the first week of the credit period.

A moment's misgiving slowed his step as he re-entered the working area. Pamela might be hard to find. Even in the prevailing atmosphere of laissez faire he could hardly check every rump for three moles in a cluster.

A blonde in an alcove, sitting alone in a sketchy tabard of gold ivy leaves, gave him a supple beckon. Chivalry had its protocol. He leaned in to say, "Not tonight, Jocasta, I'm going to the wars." Pamela Harte said, "What are you on about, you big ape? It's me."

"It is I, surely."

"My God. If you don't know who you are, it's time we got out of here."

Diment gave it up. He said. "Well if you want to stay pig ignorant, why should I bother? Move it along, you're drunk enough. Come home with Horace and I'll show you my antique."

Pamela Harte looked round for the party of the third part. "Horace?"

"I am he."

"I've never been propositioned by a Horace. It has a dubious ring. How do I know I won't end up manacled in a sleazy garret?"

Diment grabbed the nearest wrist and hauled her into the thoroughfare. A few couples were dancing in the free space, faces blank, only moving below the knee to the incessant beat. They threaded a way out, Pamela trailing at arm's length.

In the small porch, with the clamor muted and the air partially pure, Diment said, "Did you fix your benefactress so that she won't be out yelling for legal redress any minute now?"

"Benefactor, actually."

The fresh air had killed the grammarian in Diment. "Not me. The girl you took the trousseau from. Did I tell you it suits you? You're a credit to take out."

She let it ride until the outer door sliced shut behind them and the astringent dawn wind made the statement a sober truth. "Benefactor. I wanted to be businesslike, so I stood just inside the door and hit the first person through with this blaster." She reversed it and held it as a club by the barrel to make a telling visual aid. "Then this girl, as I thought, dropped full length and I was sorry. It seemed all wrong. But when I got the wig off and this tabard, it was a man. I know it isn't logical, but I was glad then that I'd hit him. Who would he be with—a man or another girl?"

"Well if he was with a girl dressed as a man, they'd both be disappointed. Or would they? I can't work it out. While there are gorgeous, straight female types like yourself in the world, that's enough for a simple man to think about."

"Is this 'Horace' flattery or a considered opinion?"

Diment had found the right shuttle in the rank and was opening the hatch. He made no reply until they had risen to the first radial flightway. Then Pamela had a hand on his arm and was pointing through the plexiglass panel at their feet. Jogging along the esplanade four abreast, a platoon of black security androids was coming in from its fruitless mission to the point. Every fifty meters one peeled off the stick, turned through ninety degrees, and started off again toward the city.

Where human operators would have been stirred to baffled rage, they were unmoved, notional faces impassive. One avenue had been checked out. It was negative. They would go without fatigue and without stop until they found what they were looking for.

Pamela Harte shivered, rustling her ivy leaves.

Taking first things first, Diment said, "How can

anybody say what is true and what is not true? We are not the same people that we were a month ago. Next month who knows what we will be? Except that the basic building bricks are the same and we can't deviate too far. As of now, to use an old word that I only partly understand, I love you."

Pamela Harte had taken her wig off with a sure instinct that this was no time for dissimulation. Her dark head was still damp and smelled vaguely of seaweed as she moved in on the squab and lodged it comfortably on the pilot's shoulder.

Diment picked up the beam for residential block 29 and locked on the auto pilot.

Yolanda Raidney—a personal emissary from the outfield to home base—decanted herself from her gold and green, long-range shuttle with a sinuous twist and walked with deedy steps up the ramp to the porch of the admin silo.

Urania City was, as always, a satisfying place to return to. Set in isolation on the southern slope of high moorland, it was, like its citizens, a miracle of functional design.

Isolation was deliberate. Although its people infiltrated every council in the Western Hemisphere Association of Regional Governments, there was no two-way traffic.

Planned as a hexagon with a containing wall, bland folds of brown moor as a bezel, it glowed with color in the early morning light like a huge jewel. It was a setting for a precise count of one hundred thousand men and women, on a fifty-fifty basis, permanently settled at the age they had chosen, undeviating and undisturbed by the clamor of the young or the querulous demands of the old.

Returning to it had some of the ambiance of a

proconsular visit to the eternal city. Except that no unwashed plebs lined its immaculate avenues to drop fag ends and shout a sentimental welcome with beery breath. What satisfaction there was had to come from the mind, and Yolanda Raidney's was well fixed to supply it, an illustration of the old adage that a filthy mind is a perpetual feast.

The smooth Raidney map was glowing with inner pleasure as she crossed the lobby, stopped at a hexagonal kiosk, and filled out a visiting slip with an electronic stylus.

Although it was early in the day and first light was only now flooding in at the panoramic window spreads, she only had to wait the forty-five seconds it took for the reception sensors to scan the data, call up the pipe, get a clearance and a ready invitation, and say, in a voice that came sibilantly from nowhere in particular, "You are to go up, Miss Raidney. The Chief Organizer will be happy to see you at once."

It came as no surprise. She clearly believed it was no more than her due to be given instant audience with the most powerful individual in the Western Hemisphere, which, indeed, was the civilized world.

Round-the-clock activity was the norm in Urania City. Sleep was not needed and was only taken at rare intervals as a novelty or to research into the simple habits of undeveloped man.

The hexagonal admin silo was one of six tower cores, each placed centrally in equilateral triangles formed by the three diagonal trunks of the city.

The elevator plucked her at fantastic speed from the ground floor to the slowly revolving platform top which housed the Chief Organizer's suite. As the floor of the cage moved out to take her on her journey through a lush anteroom laid out like a botanical garden, two bright steel special androids fell in at either side and escorted her to a multileaf door which sliced open like an iris eye shutter.

A voice of penetrating sweetness said, "Come in, my dear," and followed it, after a pause, with, "You can leave us now."

The two androids wheeled away. No slouch at recognizing what was going on, Miss Raidney knew she had been given every refined check that could be made down to the last tissue in her sling purse. Unless she was clean as a hound's tooth, she would not have gotten this far. The small hesitation had been for some undetectable signal of clearance to pass.

The Chief Organizer, however, came forward in unaffected welcome and was matching her smile for smile, hand extended in a traditional welcome.

They were matched also in height. They could have been twin sisters. But the satrap of the Western World currently done up in a female package on the reasonable precept that a change is as good as a rest, had very widely spaced blue eyes and a more opulent figure, which was open to any curious eye, behind a translucent, rose madder shift with a broad belt of hexagonal platinum links.

The Chief Organizer kept hold of the Raidney hand, led her to a large, double-ended sofa, and they sank together into its deep foam upholstery.

Incongruously the conversation was strictly businesslike and bore no relation to the action. The Chief Organizer said, "I have studied the reports. I do not think there is any cause for alarm, but your section was wise to treat the matter seriously. The specials have already set out. It will not take long to stabilize the situation. Now that we are comfortable, you can give me your opinion and tell me what you think a man like this Diment is likely to do next. How is it I never met you before? I sense a sadistic quality in your mind which is very interesting. I must find a use for it in our organization. Every talent should be deployed to advantage."

Yolanda Raidney acknowledged a compliment where it was due. As a personnel adviser, she could appreciate management technique in action better than most. Her small red tongue licked briefly at her shapely lip and she settled herself like a well-groomed cat for any collateral pleasure that might stem from the mission.

At Horace Johnson's roomy pad, Roger Diment came in from the balcony for the second time and looked at the sleeping girl. The spirit of the absent Graphics Consultant moved him to kneel down beside the divan and shift her ringlet for better effect so that it lay like a shining rope in the convenient hollow between her breasts.

She was deeply asleep and he knew he ought to waken her, but he was trying to weigh up the angles and on balance it seemed better that they should split up. She might as well have another hour in the sack. If she was awake, she would argue, and the logic of it might not stand.

He fixed a pinger to blast off at ten hundred hours and found an ivorine writing tablet to leave a message. "Fix yourself some coffee, but don't be tempted to eat. Every last can has that barley sheaf on it. I've gone ahead, eventually to the museum; but I have a call to make on the way. May take some time. See you there. Take care of yourself. Watch for any bright steel type android. I've seen one below in the street. Looks to be a special job. Love. Roger."

He chocked it delicately with the ringlet and got himself to the hatch.

Horace Johnson was a snappy dresser, and it had taken some research in the closet to find a set of unobtrusive gear. He had settled for brown slacks and a green turtleneck sweater. One blaster was shoved in his waistband, the other was beside the bed for Pamela.

In the corridor, Diment felt more alone than any time he could remember. He had given a hostage to fortune and as of now there was no comfort in it.

With an effort of will, he shrugged it off, forced himself to close the door without looking back, and padded silently along the corridor for the elevator trunk.

The cage had dropped three levels before he was joined by other commuters. He had the blaster grip in his hand, but there was no need to use it. Two men and a girl stepped in, looked at him without any curiosity, and stood in silence as the cage continued its drop. Thinking back, he reckoned he would have done the same at that stage. There was a definite stifling of inquisitiveness in the public at large. It was "I'm all right Jack" on a cosmic scale. It would have been all the same if he had been a two-headed dwarf. Unless he had actually nipped a piece out of somebody's flank, there would be no recation.

It made the mission he was on all the more vital.

According to a regional map on Horace Johnson's wall, which had triggered off the decision, Regional Farm Seven lay twenty kilometers distant to the South West of Barnston City.

He picked up a shuttle and checked its fuel gauge. Horace had drawn a new capsule on the first of the month and it was hardly more than one-third used. He had a range of six hundred kilometers.

Diment imagined a map with a circle drawn on that radius. That brought in a lot of places he could visit on a one-way no-return trip. For a count of five, he debated whether or not to go back, dig out Pamela Harte, and make a run for it. He imagined the sweep of a pair of dividers over the chart. Mostly over sea, then hitting Thorshaun in the Faeroes, Bergen, Frederikshaven, Hamburg, Frankfurt, Strasbourg and meeting the coast again at Bordeaux, with many other cities lying inside the ring.

But then, when you had seen two you had seen them all. Traveling with the Barnston City Rifle Team had proved that. Slice it where you liked, the Western Federation had a uniform pattern and danced to the same jig. There was no hiding place.

Also there was Carl Borsey, making his personal statement at the sea wall. Only one more unit joining the majority group of the dead, but either that was important, or nothing was important and he might as well walk along to the nearest guard with his wrists out for the gyves.

The chances were it would come to that; but while he was still a free agent he had to use his time for what he saw to be good. Even if it should turn out to be a false light it was the only light he had.

Diment took the shuttle to intercity freeway six and called for clearance.

An android traffic clerk in the control tower asked for detail and Diment shoved Horace Johnson's identity tab into the scanning slot in the console. He also asked, pitching his voice high in what he hoped would carry a Graphics ambiance, "What's the problem? I have a schedule to meet. Surely there's no traffic delay at this time.?"

"No problem. All outgoing cars have to be checked. Transmit a front face picture."

Diment was already rummaging in the tray below the console and fished out the car's service book. There was a four-centimeter-square identity mug shot of its owner on the cover and he held it over the scanning eye for a brief exposure. Then he said, "God. It's gone again. I've had to have that fixed twice in as many weeks. Did you get that? Came on and went off. There's an intermittent fault. Hold on, I'll try it again."

"It will not be necessary. Clearance granted."

Diment expanded the chart spread to its maximum, which gave a twenty-kilometer range. Regional Farm Seven lay left of the freeway with its own grid of surface roads and a blue hatching round its perimeter. That meant it could not be crossed by unauthorized traffic.

Jutting into the plain, half a kilometer beyond the far border, was a high escarpment and a low range of hills. He would have to edge round into that area, leave the car, and use his feet.

When the farm was in direct vision, optimism took a knock. It was bigger then he had expected. Grainfields, ribbed by dual tracks to carry tiller-combines, stretched out in kilometer-long strips. Silos and highrise cattle pens were grouped in units of five like bulbous gray stars on a colored cloth. Low geodesic domes were sited like stranded jellyfish all round the perimeter. As he watched, one of the tiller machines, straddling the whole width of a strip and running on two bogies powered by linear motors, began a slow run spraying a fine, white dust. In the center, a squat control tower with a vast plexiglass dome was clearly the pivot of the operation.

Whatever he hoped to find would be there, but it would take time. Also, he realized that any value in the exercise would only be gained if it was not known that he had been there.

It was a tall order. Diment passed the farm and took the first filter off. Then he followed an old surface road and flew at zero height into a thicket.

When he left the shuttle, he reckoned he would be a lucky man if he saw it again.

CHAPTER SEVEN

Pamela Harte heard heavy breathing almost vertically overhead, kept her eyes closed to postpone the pleasure of opening them, said "Roger," in a tone compounded of delight and reaffirmation of the position she was in, and stretched out her arms to lock them round his head and assist component orientation.

Heavy breathing could belong to anybody in the context, but Horace Johnson's pin-cushion head had an ambiance all its own. Without being a dermomorph, she could tell at a touch she was grappling with a ringer. Eyes flicked wide open and focused on a stranger. She said "Eek" and wriggled like any startled eel out of the nest.

Horace Johnson's long session at The One-Handed Clap had not sharpened his reflexes. He was still looking at the girl-shaped void under his arms when Pamela Harte spoke for the third time. By the only bit of good fortune knocking about, she had stood briefly on the blaster beside the bed, recognized it, scooped it up, and was feeling as much ahead of the game as any freshly wakened nude in an alien bed could expect.

She said nastily, "What have you done with Roger?"

It was a difficult question. His blank look was, however, a sufficient answer.

As far as he could think coherently at all, he reckoned he had grounds for some explanations himself. He had borrowed a set of coveralls and made the return journey on foot, putting down his dilemma to the bizarre sense of fun of the party he had been with. The concierge had given him a duplicate key to his apartment. He had been leaning over Pamela as much in a spirit of inquiry as of lust.

Starting at the beginning, he said petulantly, "Who's Roger? I never heard of him. What would I want with your Roger?"

He took a step forward and the blaster lined up on his sternum.

Pamela Harte said, "That's near enough."

Bemused or not, he could still recognize when not to push his luck. He stopped, hands by his sides, and conversation died the death. Research had long established that for social comfort it was desirable to talk with a person you could see entirely or not at all. He could not reasonably expect to see any more of Pamela Harte; but he could have told the investigators that they had it all wrong. It was the least satisfactory dialogue he had ever been in. To check out the alternative aspect of the report, he closed his eyes. That satisfied the other research requirement, but the voice sounded no less gritty as Pamela Harte said, "Turn around and walk slowly over to that closet."

Facing away from the blaster and taking it real slow, he heard the step up close behind. Suddenly, there seemed less real menace in the situation. She was just a kook, trying it on for laughs. If he let her get away with it, he would never live it down.

With his hand going for the latch he changed direction and whipped round to grab for the gun.

Mere reflex tightened her finger on the activator stud and an intense asterisk of white flame blossomed briefly on his chest. Horace Johnson had become a Wayfarer ahead of schedule.

Hardened to the violent life and illogically blaming Diment for putting her in a situation where she had to do it, Pamela Harte felt no immediate remorse. She grabbed a psychedelic cover from the bed and spread it over the corpse.

If Residential Block 29 followed normal procedures, it would not be long before the daily room service got under way. Well, it would give them something to think about as they filled their trash can. Like Diment, she rummaged in the locker for something to wear and settled for a candy striped anorak. Crotch length on the late Graphics man, it dropped to mid thigh and would hide her ivy leaves.

When she was ready to go, she put the hood up and drew it close with a purple thong. Only then, looking back at the quiet room with its owner visible as a molded shape under the embroidered cloth, did she think of the enormity of what she had done.

She was alone. She was branded with the mark of Cain. Now she could see Johnson's eyes as they registered the diamond moment of death. Nothing in her cossetted past had prepared her for this situation. For a moment she thought that she should go along to the precinct security post and give herself up.

But to whom? To androids? To a system that had her kind in a net? There would be no justice in that. It would be simple suicide. With the impact of revelation she saw that living and struggling were two sides of the same coin. She put it into words and said it aloud to convince herself. "Living is struggling. You have to learn to like it."

That was something she could say to Diment. By giving up struggling and passing every decision to electronics aids, mankind had sold the past. Mind had been externalized and body was off on its own kick, which had gotten it to a cozy rabbit run with the executioners setting their guns at the pop holes.

The dumb shape under the sheet when rightly considered was only half a man. She was only a half Cain.

Guilt rationalized by a generous percentage, she walked off with a firm step.

In the lobby, she saw a tall, silvery android crossing the porch and went over to the check board as though about to change an in-out tab. Miniaturized on the polished disks, she watched him multiplied to a squad, cross to the kiosk, and begin a methodical workout on the information panel. Maybe it was routine or maybe they had a lead on Horace Johnson.

Heart notching up to andante, she walked casually to the long spread of plexiglass double-leaf doors and stepped out into mild sunshine.

In the Barnston City museum complex, Harry Bedall was a worried man. Even Amenophis's daughter, fairly pushing her unguent jar with a disarming smile, did nothing to take his mind off the situation.

He could see both sides of the coin and had every sympathy with the minority group that opted for the quiet life. It was, after all, the way he had played it himself for years. But he knew for a truth that it could not go on forever. Their enclave was a microcosm and followed the basic rule of the larger society outside the gate in any age. Human institutions were dynamic, forward or back, no standing still for long or they decayed and fell apart at the seams.

In some sense he had been going forward in setting it up at all. But for the last few years, in spite of what he had said to Diment, he had been aware that he had developed the closed group as far as it would go.

He also saw that a Founding Father could not rely on loyal gratitude for ever. Give a man his life and he wanted to use it, sooner or later, for his own ends. Joe Brogan's faction, for instance, was getting stronger all the time. A few more votes and they could get their views accepted by the very Council he had created as a democratic front for his own policy. As Rousseau had it, the majority might be wrong, nevertheless it was always right.

For godsake, how a neat phrase could conceal the truth. That kind of thinking had gotten the world where it was. That and the defeatist mush of the late twentieth century, where every leading authority had fallen over backward to be tolerant and pretend that there was no qualitative difference between one human act and another. No absolute value scale separating "Pop Goes the Weazel" and Beethoven's Fifth, between graffiti and Botticelli's marine Venus, between *Portnoy's Complaint* and *Ulysses*. If it existed it was an okay thing in its own right, no better and no worse than anything else. The only parameter was reality.

Lydia Brunswick, tired of pounding corn on a quern, crossed the Bronze Age set and prodded the seer with her pestle. "For godsake, Harry, snap out of it. You're making me nervous. The customers'll think you've slipped a gear and call for a repair crew. Polish an arrow head or sacrifice that virgin to the great brooding spirit of the grove. What's eating you?"

"It's too long since we heard from Diment. I was a fool to let him go."

"You're no fool and you know it. Most people agree with you. Nothing lasts forever. You had no choice."

"It's come too soon. We're not strong enough. Once they know, they could clear us out of here in half an hour."

"That's not Harry Bedall talking. Where's your libido?"

She moved in closer, until she was nudging pneumatically against his bare chest, a therapy that short-circuited the internal debate.

He said, "Come into my conical hut and see if you can find it."

A clear treble from the barrier asked, "What are those two Ancient Britons going into that beehive for?"

An android curator said smoothly, "The woman has been grinding corn. Now she will hang a grid of warp threads from the straight branch of a tree, holding the ends firm with little blobs of clay. Then she will weave a piece of coarse cloth using a simple shuttle to carry the weft. It will be used as a blanket or to trade with the traveling merchants for a copper ring."

Lydia Brunswick said philosophically, "I'll help you to look for it another time. A woman's work is never done. It surprises me that the race ever survived and multiplied."

Later in the midday break there was general

agreement that the visitor count for the morning had hit an all time high. The museum had not been packed to the door, but business was certainly looking up.

Geof Konstad took a pessimist's view. "It's because they know the place is coming down. You only value a thing when you're losing it, as the apothecary's daughter said. Mark my words, we'll be run off our feet from now on. Then they'll close it and the wreckers'll move in."

"That doesn't follow." His neighbor, in the group stretching their legs in the lower gallery, was Joe Brogan. "It doesn't follow at all. If attendance goes up they'll see the need for it. It's in our favor. We're all set here for as long as we like, provided nobody goes out of line and draws attention. I tell you, I hope Diment's lot have bought it. A man like that only brings trouble."

Bedall, having got his libido back, spoke up for the absent. "That kind of talk gets us nowhere. We all agreed that what they were trying to do was an okay thing. I'm more sure of it than ever. If they're not back in twenty-four hours I want volunteers for a search. I have an idea we should start nearer home. Somewhere at this end of the conveyer line there has to be a control point. Somebody looks over that harvest of tripes and says where it has to go."

Carol Greer said, "It goes to the medicenters, surely. That's what guarantees thirty trouble-free years for the man in the street. Or woman."

Bedall said, "That's what we always believed, Carol. But think back. How many people do you know who went in for transplant surgery? I bet you could count them on the fingers of one hand. Unless they're being stockpiled against the Last Trump, there's no need for all that."

A muted pinger sounded the countdown for the afternoon session and they dispersed to their mansions.

First foot over the threshold as the time lock came off was Pamela Harte. She had made a long detour on foot and was ready for any role that promised a chair or a bed. A silver android standing in open concealment with a group of modern statuary in the square watched her in and extruded a small antenna from behind his left aural sensor. He called base, using internal circuits and making no sounds that could be picked up by the few passers-by.

It was direct transfer to the computer in the Organizer's headquarters for Barnston City. Bedall would have been pleased to find confirmation for his hunch. Barely five hundred meters from where he sat at the door of his conical hut, a ticker tape extruded from an output slot and was read off by the newly promoted Controller for the region. "One of the wanted persons has now entered the museum complex. It is the woman. Timed 1330 hours. Special Unit Zero three six. What are your instructions?"

Yolanda Raidney, standing beside the top hand, with all the authority of a special envoy said, "We should wait. Eventually the man will return. Then we will have them all."

To pass the time she took Diment's ivorine tablet out of her pocket and refreshed her memory of the simple text.

In the crowded minutes of wakening it had fallen from its warm hollow and never having seen it, Pamela Harte had not missed it. A room service android had moved with creditable speed to call up the precinct guard to look at Horace, and a close search for the murder weapon had discovered the directive between the sheets.

Following an all stations call to report anything unusual to the new task force, it had been handed on to the Controller as evidence. Though not before the station sergeant had copied the text for his log.

Speaking to his junior at the desk he had said, "We're looking for a right one here, Jack. Every can you ever see has a barley sheaf on it. If he sticks to that he'll starve himself to death and save us all a lot of grief."

The Raidney computer let the data lie about in its association unit for a short count and gave lateral thinking a chance.

The Chief Organizer's confidence was not misplaced. When it passed over the threshold to decision-making areas, it was tagged with a whole raft of annotation. She said suddenly, "Of course, they were in the food supply areas. They identified the source as Regional Farm Seven. This Diment is far from stupid. He has understood that additives are introduced. He warns the woman not to eat. Which suggests that they both know of a source of untreated food. Where does the food for the museum come from?"

The Controller, conscious that he should have worked it out for himself, said reluctantly, "There is a preparation plant on the site. Also a small livestock unit. It existed before we took over. It has never been thought necessary to change it, since the products were all disposed of as waste."

"But it would support a small community."

"Your point is taken. But the museum has been checked repeatedly. No human fugitives have ever been found there."

She let it go and went on another tack, "Diment has not been seen in the city and the specials have made a thorough check. I believe he has gone to follow his line of inquiry at the farm."

"That is unlikely. He could not walk that distance and every outgoing car has been scanned."

"How many?"

"Only traffic control can answer that."

"I'd like to ask them. I want to see a playback of every scan."

"They have had his picture for matching."

"Nevertheless there could be something they have overlooked."

The Controller hesitated, a momentary indecision that was not lost on the court favorite. Then he thought wisely that it would do no harm to get her off his back on a routine chore that might take a lot of time. Also, with some luck, it could be fruitless and take the eternal smile off her face.

He played a complicated sequence on his pianola and spoke shortly to the traffic superintendant, "Have the station log played back through this channel. Start from the point when the check was put on."

To Yolanda Raidney he said, "I will switch it to the duplicate screen in the anteroom. Then you can give it your undivided attention."

In her absence he got on with his own program, calling the special squad section leader and telling him to recall his scattered detail and have them seal off the museum complex. Having no faith in the Raidney reading of the situation, he added, "They are to remain concealed. Do nothing to alarm the man Diment. When he is inside the museum, we will move in and settle this business once and for all. He is armed with a phasor, but he is required for interrogation so take care not to kill him. Use grade three paralysis."

Yolanda Raidney, who had left the door open so that she could follow the action, called through, "And the woman who was his companion. The same applies. There is some unfinished business I have to attend to. They should be interrogated together. It will be interesting to see at what point they will betray each other."

She had stopped the tape to add her useful gloss and prodded the restart with an elegant forefinger. Then she was looking at Horace Johnson's close-cropped head with as much surprise as Pamela Harte had done in an earlier sequence, though with less emotional overload.

Vindication had come her way and she lost no time spreading the good word.

"Controller."

"What is it?" He thought it was a little hard that his first independent command should have brought him such a pushing assistant. He had never liked working with her when she had stuck to her last as personnel adviser. Then she had been Magnes's headache. Maybe that was why he had settled for gray hair.

"Would you just look at this face."

The tone was critical as though she had found a slug in her chef's salad. Johnson's ka, if it was still flitting about the city, might have toppled a chair in pique.

The Controller said, "We both saw Diment. No disguise could make him look like that one. How very ugly some of them look."

His helpmeet said impatiently, "Of course I know this is not Diment. It is the man whose clothes he used. This one was found dead in his apartment."

The flaw in the argument was obvious and the Controller was on to it in a flash. "Then he could not be piloting a shuttle. You must be mistaken."

"Look more closely at the texture. There is no depth. This is a flat picture which has been slipped into the scanner."

"You could be right." In the circumstances it was a generous admission.

"I am certainly right. The car left on Freeway six. That passes close beside Regional Farm Seven. Diment has gone there. Give me an escort of three specials and I will bring him back."

That was an easy one, the Controller remembered. Diment's phaser. He had no chance in the long term, but he might well get in a close shot at the personnel adviser.

He said mildly, "Do that, Miss Raidney. Go and bring him in."

Diment, diminished to an ant on one gigantic running rail of a tiller-combine, was less than a hundred meters from his objective.

He was walking in a concrete gulley beside a running rail, blinkered by sheer sides that went half a meter above his head. It made for single-mindedness. There was only one way to go.

Off load, his mind ranged over the incredible organization of the farm. In some ways it was the feudal system of cultivated strips updated. But any vassal switched to it would be hard pressed to find anything to do with his hoe. Each hundred-meter width was straddled by a latticed gantry operated from a central bridge. One ponderous run down the length completed a cycle of work, turning the fertile loam, sterilizing, sowing, feeding, weeding, harvesting, without any weighty body interfering

with the fine tilth. It could even spread and re-
cover a fine transparent film to beat the vagaries of
the climate. Yield per hectare was predictable,
standardized, calculated to the last ear.

In his few millennia of progress, *Home sapiens*
had gotten the environment sewed up. But to what
end? He was no happier. Diment saw with the force
of revelation that happiness could not be reached by
direct assault. It had to be taken by stealth, when
even the seeker had forgotten it as a precise objective. It was a by-product of other activity. In the
last analysis the man was better off chipping patiently with his adze, thinking of Meg keeping a little
something hot in the hovel, than having all the time
in the world to anesthetize himself at The One-
Handed Clap.

Maybe there was a middle course to give the best
of both worlds. Speculation died the death. He had
reached journey's end. A massive carriage with a
flexible skirt to conserve air pressure blocked the
way ahead.

A little sabotage would be easy enough. No doubt
the heavy gear was lifted so that it would slide
almost frictionless on a cushion of air along the
guide bar. Break a feed pipe and it would grind
itself to an expensive halt.

But then he remembered that he wanted it left so
that his visit was not recorded.

Diment heaved himself cautiously on to the
narrow deck of the long trolley and lay out along a
cross rib of the gantry itself. The control tower was
unexpectedly close, rearing its slab-sided solar walls
from a paved apron not twenty meters distant.

Except for the overall trim cleanliness of the place
and the movement of the tiller-combine farther
down the line, the farm could have been deserted.

For that matter there would be no need for many operators wandering on the site. Sensors buried in the soil would make a continuous report on conditions of temperature, moisture, and nutrient level. The whole place could be operated by one or two specialists. Organizers, probably. Like the late Magnes.

Nothing moved. He eased himself along the beam until he was outside the gulley, went down to a full arm stretch, and dropped lightly to the parquet.

In the open he felt very vulnerable. His skin crawled, recognizing that it would be in the front line for any charge of buckshot from a farmer defending his own against a prowler. But there was no challenge.

Out of the acoustic cage of the gulley, there was a living hum as though the whole area was using power.

Diment dusted himself off and forced himself to walk slowly across the courtyard. He rounded two of the tower's six sides before he found a deep covered porch and a way through to the inside. No mixen here. There was a muted hospital ambiance, an antiseptic smell; a carry over from the worldwide crisis of many centuries back when microbiologists had come near to halting the life force in its tracks by their cultures of anti-life organisms.

Off the hall there were five doors, six counting the entrance, and in the center a reception kiosk organized round two faces of the hexagonal elevator trunk. It was unmanned, as though there was no call for the service; clear enough evidence that the general public was not encouraged to visit.

Checking through viewing ports in two doors, Diment saw standard office spreads with clerical grade androids built into the fixed furniture. Back at the kiosk, he found a schematic diagram of the complex and let his head save his feet.

There were eight floors and a penthouse structure for the presiding Organizer and his control bridge. Every floor was divided six ways into identical office units, each labeled with the name of a city in the region. Below ground there was a terminus for monorail freight cars, barns for the raw product, processing plant, and at the lowest level, an area hatched in purple with the legend *Biochemical Division*.

There was the sense of moving about an enchanted palace. It would have been all one if a courteous arm had materialized from the brickwork to take his hat and umbrella. It was difficult to equate the automated plant with any intention of evil, but it was there somewhere in the heap, sinister but streamlined into a program.

Five floors down, at basement level, Diment stepped from the cage into a reek of formaldehyde stronger than anything yet. The landing was a glass cubicle that projected out like a box in a theatre over the workshop floor. White-topped lab benches lined the walls of the working area on three sides. The fourth was filled by a long console and an organ array of piping that ran up through the ceiling to carry the product to where it would do most good. In the center a squat silo ran a fan of feed pipes every which way.

Diment had a moment's regret for a misspent youth. No crash course in chemistry, however brief, would have him walking confidently to the right tap in that lot. Nor was there anybody to ask or persuade.

He slid back a glass door and went down a steep companion as if into a ship's engine room. Noise battered at his head, metallic clicks as the silo turned, lifted and reversed. The slurp and suck of unseen liquids finding their own level, the sandpaper grind of granules in a dry mix. At the same time, he felt that he had put himself definitively in a trap.

Every work head on the factory floor was making a compound of up to half a dozen ingredients and sending them on by vacuum suction to be dispensed by the mastermind at the far end.

He went slowly along, not sure what he was looking for. Trying to reason it out, with the din making it difficult to think at all, he reckoned that the answer would be simple rather than complex. Most of the products would be nutrients, cattle food, fertilizer, growth stimulants. For the human crop, the additive would have to go into a variety of different foods and the lowest common denominator would be a clear liquid, like water, which could be absorbed without giving rise to a color change or a texture change that would be rejected as a novelty.

There were five work heads dealing in liquids, but only one fulfilled all the criteria.

This one was doing a blending job from two liquid sources, with a long white cylinder in a clip hanging over the mixing vat and injecting a measured shot into every liter.

The cylinder itself was unusual in the setting since everything else was built in as part of the fabric. Under the bench there was a stack of six, all full, waiting to be brought into use.

From the level gauge of the working model, Diment saw that it was half full. The small squirt every other minute would give it a long life. But eventually it would have to be changed. The process was simple enough to be automated. Why not then?

It was a key feature, too important to be left to chance, even the one chance in a million of mechanical failure.

Diment looked around for a plain sink unit and found one ten meters along the bench. He carried the cylinders one at a time, opened their valves, and set them to drain. When the first one was empty, he half filled it with water and carried it back to the work head, then he switched it for the one in position and carried that to empty and refill.

When it was done and the cylinders were re-stacked, he tore a piece out of his coveralls and wiped up every last drip. Sweating like a pig and half demented by the mechanical clatter that kept the beat without a variation of tone or time, he looked at his handiwork and found it good.

He was halfway to the foot of the companion when another thought struck him and he forced himself to go back. He heaved out the top cylinder and checked it for any sign of a point of origin. When he had it, it meant nothing. A small plate welded onto the base flange said *Urania City Division U4*.

Whatever it was, there was a case for passing it on. For the first time in the sequence, he thought about Pamela Harte and the group in the museum. He should get back there and see if anybody knew anything about it.

When the cubicle door closed off the noise he was even more sure of it and suddenly glad to have a base and a clan identity.

Diment went rapidly through the upper hall, paused in the porch to check the ground, saw it unchanged, and sauntered out to his long concrete furrow. He had hauled himself onto the platform of the tiller-combine when a green and gold shuttle flashed briefly across the sun, hovered fifty meters over the apron, and dropped like a free-standing elevator to a neat four point landing.

It was still flexing on its jacks when its hatches whipped smartly away and Yolanda Raidney with her three aides spilled out in a copybook police-raid gambit.

One stood by the car. The other two fell in behind the deedy redhead and followed her at a fast walk round the corner and out of sight.

It was all so quick that if Diment had not been looking that way, he would have missed it and gone on not knowing that old friends were looking him up.

Moving a centimeter at a time, he edged away and dropped into the gulley.

Baffled by the thick walls, the dynamo hum cut off and he had the illusion of being alone. He had gone two hundred meters at a steady trot when the impossibility of getting clear struck him with the force of a blow.

There was no doubt that they had come to the farm looking for him. Only Pamela knew where he had gone. Somehow or other they had got on to Horace Johnson and had picked her up at the apartment.

Searching the farm would be easy. Even now, very now, they could be checking out all the possible approach roads. Long before he reached the end of this track they would be on to it. There was no cover outside.

He would be caught leaving the scene. So they would want to know what he had done. Eventually they would get it out of him.

On the other hand, if they thought he had just arrived, they would not ask.

What he had managed to do might pay off. It might start something if people began to ask questions.

He began to walk slowly the way he had come. He would be discovered approaching the control tower with intent. No android would suspect anything so illogical.

CHAPTER EIGHT

Pamela Harte concluded a well-told tale to a representative group on the lower gallery. Bedall, with half his attention focused on the telltale for advance warning of visitors on the way up the ramp, could only say, "Well don't worry. Nip upstairs. Settle in that astronaut tableau for a spell and get some rest. Diment knows what he's doing. He'll be back."

Joe Brogan said, "Unless he's skipped out of the region. He's got a car. Maybe he's cut his losses. It was a stupid move from first to last. Are you sure Borsey was dead? If they got to him, he'd have to tell about this place."

Pamela Harte gave him a slow burn that would have got through anybody else's skin. She was saved an answer by a subdued bleep from Bedall's simple hut. Moving off at a run, she heard Brogan say to whoever was still listening, "How do we know she wasn't followed? Diment might have sold out. I don't like it."

Having time to think, with her ringlet swinging like a dark pendulum as she ran, she realized that it could be so. What did she know about Diment when all was said? How was he any different from the men she had known in pre-Wayfarer affairs? The fact that they were shadows and he was very vivid was only an accident of timing. Recall was better because he was recent.

She imagined him in the car already crossing the coast. All that grooming talk about love was strictly for the birds.

Steps slowed to a halt. If that was true, nothing was important. The sooner the androids moved in and settled the business, the better. The whole point of the system was made. They deserved no more. But he could at least have left a message to say what he was doing.

But then you had to trust people. It worked both ways. Whatever was said, she ought to go on believing in Diment until there was contrary proof.

She began running again. It was like one of those ancient riddling trials, a test. She had to keep an open mind. But then she didn't have an open mind. He was there in the very fabric of it, like a fifth column.

The astronaut group was more receptive. She settled in the capsule with a spare suit from the locker and talked to them over the intercom. They were some of the younger men with one trim redhead from the last-but-one Wayfarer group.

Grant Chadwick, a man she had seen in the long house but had not previously spoken to, a large quiet character who kept out of group politics, fell into the jargon of the period and said, "Brogan goofed on that. Diment'll be back. But we're moving to a splashdown. I reckon we should break out of here and pick up some cars and blast off right out of the region. There's land enough on the neutral zone without crossing into Eastern Hem. Even then its an empty quarter."

Roy Stanwick, another fringe member who was content to bide his time, turning on the revolving platform of a radio telescope, said, "But sterile. Eastern Hem's supposedly still radioactive."

"How do we know that? I read somewhere that the effect wears off in time and God knows it's had a few centuries."

Stanwick said, "Hold it, Chad. There's something coming through on the emergency link. It's Bedall. Very quiet, I can hardly get it."

Each gallery had one relay point and the astronaut tableau was the natural outlet for the top deck. A flasher on the capsule's instrumentation spread was winking ABORT. Pamela Harte pushed back the hatch and leaned out. Bedall had never expected to use it for real and could hardly believe that the end game had started, but two entirely new androids had appeared in the lower gallery and were using a brand new technique to sort the quick from the dead.

In the first tableau Dawn Man was represented waving a thigh bone at an ominous sky and keeping predators out of his rock dwelling with a small fire.

The predators padding about upstage were rude mechanicals. Most of the protagonists were androids. It was not an easy stint and few ever chose it except to make a break after more sophisticated employment.

Fortunately there was one, a small bowlegged oldster who liked to make use of his heavy beard and hairy chest and found few satisfactory parts higher up the time scale. Jim Kruger by name, he had heard footsteps on the ramp and had shaken his bone at the backdrop and then kicked his way through the huddle of women and children round the fire grabbing a relatively comely one and dragging her by her top knot toward the cave.

A simple, hard-working man giving of his best where another would have gone in for a postprandial nap on a skin bed, he was surprised when there was a high-pitched ping from the barrier and a smart blow on the outside of his right shoulder knocked him off balance.

Kruger was round in a flash, ready with the prepared bit about not throwing bric-a-brac at the exhibits. Two pieces of information, presented together, held him back. One was the novel aspect of the visitors. He had not seen anything like them before and the single rotating visual sensor set in the crown of their ovoid domes had a glowing intensity that was hypnotic in its effect. The other was more personal and broke the mesmeric spell they were putting out. His right arm was sticky with blood which was welling from a neat three-centimeter incision.

He dropped his mate and her head hit the rocky floor with a metallic knock. The marksman said, "He bleeds. That is one of them. Report to the Controller that we are on the right track. I will secure him."

Kruger picked up his feet and whipped into the cave mouth like a gopher into its hole. He was through a rear exit into a narrow connecting corridor behind the arras before the android had gotten one tin leg over the rail.

His report to Bedall was brief and fully supported by circumstantial evidence. His arm was red to the wrist.

Bedall wasted no time. The general alert that Stanwick was getting said, "This is it. They've started to move in. Withdraw to the roof. Keep out of sight. Bring any weapons you have."

The Organizer in control, having moved on receipt of Yolanda's signal that Diment had been contacted and would not be back, heard the report with every satisfaction. He said, "Very well. Continue. All special details will join you. Save alive at least a dozen for interrogation, but destroy any who resist. They are expendable."

In saying that her hunch had paid off and that she had Diment all buttoned up at the farm, Yolanda Raidney was ahead of fact. He was present, true; but the first silver android to drop into the gulley for a High Noon-type confrontation was melted to an obscene stump before he could return Diment's fire.

Diment was within twenty-five meters of the tiller-combine when the android appeared over the rim. Confident of superior armament, it turned its back and climbed deliberately down the trellis. Diment dropped on one knee, steadied the phasor on his forearm, and waited until it touched down. As it began to turn, he sent a thin searing beam to hit with clinical accuracy in the center of the ovoid head.

The first five seconds of impact made no difference except that the turning face was brilliantly lit. It even moved a pace along the gully with one arm coming up to aim.

The revolving eye was sending a beam on its own account as though it had collected all the energy and focused it for a return trip. Diment felt his concentration begin to slip.

Except for the bright probing beam beating at his retina, the set was going black. There was only the transfixing light left in the world. He felt himself moving forward and fell sprawled over his own knee to the concrete deck.

If he had been standing up, the fall would have knocked him cold. As it was, the rough gritty surface brought him back to the here and now. The phasor had skidded out of his hand under the running rail, he felt sick and shaken, but he was out of the hypnotic stare and waited for the return shot to tear into his back. Bitterly he reckoned that the payoff was typical of the situation they were in. He was flat on his belly in front of the man of the future.

Eyes clearing slowly, head weaving from side to side, he struggled to hands and knees. As a position, it was one up in the evolutionary scale. Given time he might even stand up.

When nothing happened he raised his head to take a look.

The android could have carried a caption—They went that-a-way. It was pointing over his head to the distant end of the track. From the shoulders up, it was a grotesque mush of melted alloys.

In the last split second of exposure to the phasor, the heat resistant outer case had passed its threshold of tolerance and inner mechanisms had liquidized and boiled through the holes.

Diment scrabbled around and found his phasor. The charge gauge was a fraction off empty. It was a strictly nonrepeatable performance.

Watching from the scanner in the farm control tower, Yolanda Raidney said, "That was very close. He cannot do it again. Since he wants to come here, we will let him come right in. To reduce his degrees of freedom I will send both guards to detour and drive him this way."

The bailiff, more at home with kilograms per

hectare than military strategy, nevertheless put his finger on a weakness in the plot. "But then we will be undefended. If he arrives here first he will kill us both."

"He is looking for information. He would not be prepared to do that. Also I have this," she opened her sling purse and took out a syringe gun. "We can watch him all the way in on your scanner. As soon as he opens the door I shall fire. It is simply a matter of reaction time with all the advantage on my side. Also that phasor must be almost empty. He will be reluctant to use the last charge."

The useful purse had another handy artifact: a palm-sized communicator which she snapped open and talked into as though calling up her sleeve.

In the scanner they saw the two special androids stop and listen. Then they took off in divergent directions at a steady run.

Diment had closed up on the headless wonder. They saw his hand go out, almost touch, and draw back. Clearly the casing was too hot to handle. He began to climb the trolley, moving slowly, obviously expecting another.

Yolanda Raidney said critically, "That is not intelligent behavior. He must know that he cannot beat the next one. It is like suicide. Why would he do that after all the efforts he has made for personal survival? Our estimate of the humans is absolutely right. In the end they are illogical. No wonder we can control them so easily."

Illogicality made an upward spiral. Diment, having gotten his head over the rim, took a long look round the set and saw that the only guards in sight were on a flanking gambit to come up from the rear. Instead of taking the open invitation to go forward for the tower, he began to climb a catwalk up the gantry toward the operating cab of the tiller-combine.

It was a clear case of the failure of behaviorist psychology to get a necklock on human motivation. Though in fairness to the Personnel Adviser, she was working without all the data.

He reasoned that he had established well enough that he was on the way in and he could afford to do something about getting out.

Diment found he was on the side opposite to the regular entry hatch and edged out along a three-centimeter flange to work across. Palms flat on plexiglass panels, he willed his center of gravity to cluster at his navel and kept his mind off the fifty-meter drop by trying to weigh up the operating console that stood in the center of the deck.

It was a complex job, but he reckoned that nine-tenths of the gear would be tied up with the changes of function. Drive mechanism could only be forward or back with maybe a speed factor if the tarpaulin had to be spread in a hurry.

At the far corner, with one hand stretched round for the coaming of the entry hatch, he took a spell and found that his knees had gone into an involuntary muscular spasm.

Down below and a hundred meters along the line the androids had completed their pincer move and were coming in, balance-walking on the inside wall of each running track.

He hauled himself round the corner and into the cab, wiping sweat off his hands and out of his eyes.

One lever marked AUTO-MANUAL spoke for itself and he shoved it to MANUAL. MOTOR was another. When he pulled it over, a low hum filled the cab and a bank of lights flicked on along the panel.

There was no time for good husbandry. Working two-handed, he went the length of the spread, heaving down every control on the board.

The gantry shivered along its length, bucked from its stops in a crash start, and lumbered off at a smart walking pace down the strip doing its thing. Shining blades clipped from their housing and chewed into the loam. Seed scattered. Drills pumped rhythmically up and down. Fertilizer billowed out in a gray cloud until it was trapped under a canopy that paid out from fixing studs in the boundary wall.

Having been ordered forward, the androids came on. Diment on his shaking bridge was grinning like a maniac and beating on the panel with both fists. The ponderous trolleys hit at the same time and he saw the silver figures heel over into the loam.

There was a jar through the deck as the cultivators did their best to get a fine tilth. A warning light joined the cluster and the vast machine slowed to allow clod breakers to drop and pound definitively at the unbreakable shells. Then he was past and thundering on down the straight.

There was nothing to see. Behind him, the transparent cover was filled with a swirling gray mist. They were well and truly planted like dragon's teeth.

From his high platform, he could see that the car on the apron had not moved and that there were no other androids about. That argued it was a small task force. The three he had seen were the lot. The ginger Organizer would be inside waiting for them to bring in his head.

For a moment he debated whether or not to reverse the gear, go back, and spike the car. But it would be pressing his luck. Better to carry on to the end of the line, pick up his own shuttle, and get to Barnston City. At least he could find out what had happened to Pamela.

He shut off every operation except forward speed. The canopy he could do nothing about. That would only wind in on reverse, but it would do no harm. No point in sabotaging the crop when he wanted it distributed without its additive.

It was a quieter run and the trolleys picked up speed. The distant copse grew as if in a zoom lens.

Harry Bedall did a rapid check of his assembled company. As a citizen army, it was not an encouraging sight. But Jim Kruger's bloody arm saved a lot of explanation. They were convinced that the emergency was real.

Grant Chadwick, who had gone straight through to the rooftop recreation area where a swivel-mounted telescope gave views of the city, brought an up-to-the-minute sitrep. "They're coming in from all round the complex. Must be twenty or more. They'll seal the first floor off and work up through the galleries."

There was silence as each took it in his own way. Though they had known that their enclave could not last for ever, it had endured long enough to gather a sense of normal life. The shock of reaching an end stop was not cushioned by euphoric drugs or subliminal suggestion. They were dying twice and the second run was with their eyes wide open.

Bedall felt the weight of leadership fold round him like a lead shroud. They were used to looking to him for a program and they were doing it now, even with an illogical hope that he could find an answer.

He stood with Lydia Brunswick, one hand on her smooth shoulder as a touchstone of the real world that lay behind the charade and said heavily. "I reckon we all knew it had to come. One day or another day it had to come. We'll give the bastards a run for their money."

Talking cleared his head and he marshaled the facts. For years, in odd minutes, he had thought how a last ditch operation could be organized on the attic. When he started again his voice had its old ring.

"Chad. Take a couple of men and jam the elevator trunk just below this floor. Nothing obvious. Just so they'll ram a cage tight. George. You and Andy go along to the ramp. Take as many as you need. Use vibrators and take a swathe out of the floor. Cut the joists underneath, then put the floor back. Fix it so that half a kilogram will break it through. Build a barrier right across just below the landing. Everybody else on the roof. I want every clear space littered with obstacles so that they can't land a car."

Pamela Harte was about to ask how Diment would get in, if he came back; but she stopped herself in time. So far, the peace-at-any-price faction had made no comment. His name would be bound to trigger off some nonproductive gloss from Brogan, for one. Instead she attached herself to Grant Chadwick's party, which was first off the mark with a bundle of duralumin tie rods from the store room.

Action was a therapy in itself. Back on load, with work to do, there was a resurge of cheerfulness in the hive. Even Russ Gribbin, a lanky harem keeper, whistled tunelessly as he split useful wedges with his scimitar.

Grant Chadwick was a neat and handy improviser. Swung out into the shaft, he lashed two tie bars across each corner, one above the other and half a meter apart. Then he took a third and fixed it to point like a spear into the roof of the rising cage.

He had finished the last one when Pamela Harte, odd-job woman and official lookout, saw the shaft shorten before her eyes. It was so quick that the cage had halved the distance before she could call out and they were pulling Chadwick over the sill when it struck.

The crash shook the landing and the cage ground itself to a halt with a handsbreadth of its shattered roof lipping over the stop. A silvery hand scrabbled through the gap and fired a random burst of tranquilizing serum into the facing wall.

Russ Gribbin, who had picked the time to see how they were getting along, stepped smartly aside, then swung his scimitar double-handed to chop at the wrist.

With fantastic reaction time the hand turned palm up and grabbed the blade by its edge. Gribbin, stuck like a paralyzed man at the end of the swing, was trying to heave it clear. When it came away, he staggered back wildly until he was brought up short by the wall.

It was all good knockabout farce, but Pamela Harte was watching the hand. It had broken out a neat half moon of Toledo steel and closed its fingers round it.

She said, awed, "Only look at that."

The metal sliver, crushed into a pellet, had been thrown out as the hand withdrew to skid over the tiles and lie at her feet.

There was no time for close analysis. A cutting flame was working along the roof of the cage. The delay was only marginal. They would be out and about in a matter of minutes.

Chadwick hooked a vibrator in his belt and

squeezed between the cage and the wall. The cutting stopped as though the androids were weighing what action was going on. Then it started again in insolent certainty. Whatever it was, they could not believe it was a serious threat.

Three sides of a flap cut through and a silver arm, shoving like a piston, cracked it back to make a meter-square manhole.

Gribbin and the other two men were backing slowly to the archway into the main hall. Pamela Harte knelt by the shaft with her ringlet hanging down like a plumb bob. She called urgently, "It's too late, Chad. Come back. They're almost through."

He had edged down under the cage and was hanging out to full-arm stretch, ripping into the floor with his vibrator. Two sides and halfway through a third and the panel began to give. He was under the opening, but he went on for another half meter, set to destroy with red hate for the androids swamping out any other thought.

They helped him with the last bit. Two standing together to heave the third through the trap, their weight was concentrated where it would do most good.

The climber upward was head and shoulders through the hole when the floor broke away.

Pamela Harte was climbing down to beat on the arm she could see and get her message home, when it was plucked from its hold.

Grant Chadwick saw her feet, and his shout "Get back" came echoing up the shaft. She hung on, sick and shaken by the suddenness of it, with one part of her mind counting out the seconds. At seven, there was a bright flash from the bottom of the pit followed by the crash of impact and a tremor that ran up the fabric under her hands.

In the main hall, she met Bedall commuting from the ramp to the roof to see how progress was. He said, "That was no trade at all. No trade at all. We can't afford to lose men like Chad."

"Is that all you can say? You're worse than Diment."

"Before we're through, those who go first could be the lucky ones. I have an idea for you and some of the younger end. Listen and don't argue. There's a disposal chute in the kitchen area. We've never used it in case it was noticed; but it falls behind the galleries with feed branches coming in from each level. It makes out on a conveyer down in the basement. If you stay on that too long you'd be ground small in a pulverizer, so you'll have to watch it."

"Why can't we all go?"

"They'd be on to it right away and then nobody'd make out. I'll pick twelve. Twelve apostles. A distinguished precedent. It's up to you to do something about the mess we've gotten into."

"I won't go."

Bedall spun her round, a hand on each shoulder, and looked her straight in the eyes. He said gently, "I'm not ordering you, Pamela, I'm asking you. Do it for me as a personal favor. You see farther through the wood than most. You and Diment between you might just come up with something."

"He could be already dead."

"You don't believe that and neither do I. What do you say?"

Noise from the ramp was notching up. There was no time for thinking it out. But Bedall's sincerity was patent and urgent. Triggered at a deep level where the life force was getting its oar in, she said, "All right. But I don't like it."

"Good girl."

He gave her a fatherly pat and hustled off, leaving her with tears welling up in her eyes. That was a novelty in itself. She could not remember crying since she was a child in one of the Initial Teaching Establishments and some dissembler had whipped off her doll to nip the emergent maternal instinct in the bud.

There was more noise from the roof, which suddenly escalated and blanked out everything else. At the far end of the hall, the ceiling had developed a massive blister, sagging like an obscene, mottled belly that split and delivered a mixture of rubble and girder work in an avalanche rumble.

The floor shook, tilted so that she had to grab a stanchion to keep on her feet, held up momentarily, and gave way in its turn. She could imagine the gathering weight would accelerate as it went on, breaking through every level until it rumbled down to the basement. Demolition was under way.

Water was cascading through the hole in a solid shaft frothing white at the edges and spilling over to wash halfway up the slope until the flow stopped and it ran back with an anti-clockwise spiral to its plug hole. The whole building shook to its foundations as the ongoing mass hammered at each succeeding level.

A minor thump, like the last small apple after a treeful falling on a cartoon picnicker, ended the sequence. It was a small triumph for the ramp party. Andy Granger, having seen two androids pick their way round the corner and drop through his Stone Age man trap, left his post and came through to see what was going on at his back.

Dust was wreathing in the air, small items were still trundling toward the hole which was picked out by a solid shaft of sunlight. Costume characters through the ages were crowding in from all sides to stand in stunned silence and look at the carnage as if seeing nothing. It was a Surrealist set that only needed a plastic nude on a bunch of twigs to have Marcel Duchamp's skeleton fidgeting its bony fingers for a crayon.

Granger, awed, said, "Holy Cow, Harry, did you have to do that?"

Bedall said shortly, "They breached the pool. Trying for a landing site. Overplayed it. But they won't be long finding another. There are two cars assing about up there. That about wraps it up. I want everybody up top. No sense in going on. We'll see how the Council deals with it."

There was no opposition. It had been obvious from the beginning. Now it was painted on the wall in banner headlines. *Mene Mene Tekel Upharsin.* Weighed and divided.

Bedall, rounding up the stragglers like a sheepdog, was also separating out the group he had chosen for the break. Pamela Harte found herself next to Carol Greer and Roy Stanwick in the storeroom behind the kitchen area. There were twelve as Bedall had promised. None looked pleased to be there.

A dark, wiry man with a thin Welsh face and a widower's peak used a handy mace to beat off the hatch cover clips which had corroded with long disuse. When the flap hinged down there was a lubricating flush of water from concealed jets and a high gamey stench as if they had broken into a medieval garderobe.

The trunking was square on a diameter of about three-quarters of a meter. It would be a tight fit for some, and Carol Greer paled a tone or two and edged away. Williams, the mace bearer, put himself in charge of the detail. He said, "Hurry it along. They can't hold out for long. We owe it to them to make this work. Pad yourself out with some cloth. Not you, Carol, you're a natural fit. Use your arms and legs as a brake, otherwise you'll be breaking the sound barrier when you hit that conveyer."

It took a couple of minutes to sort out a batting order and get the first trail breaker through the hole. Pamela Harte at number ten reckoned she could find time to see how it was outside and sidled out of line to the main hall.

It was a ruin. Made more appalling by the bright shaft of sunlight stabbing down into the pit. The vibration of her light step started a slide of rubbish down the funnel and she almost turned back. But the steps were only ten meters off and she made it at a run.

Level with the roof area she lifted her head and took a rat's-eye view of the set. One car had landed on its skids. The other was still hovering. The whole human company had been herded against the low baluster at one end of the roof with three silver androids parading in front.

As she watched, the hovering car seemed to receive a set of instructions. It moved over the heads of the guards and bore down on the human group which was still giving a more or less faithful dress parade of man's pilgrimage through the millennia.

Twin beams of eye-aching light sprang from the undercarriage and flicked like bright ropes into the crowd. Where they touched, there was nothing left. Only the skyline and the parapet and any wandering Ka given egress at all points at once.

Bitterness choked Pamela Harte's mind. What

had they done to deserve that? Gentle people. Hurting nobody. Just living longer than the system said. She went blindly back to the kitchen and found that techniques had improved. She was next in line.

There was no point in adding to the general angst. She could tell them later, if there was a later. She followed Williams's directions with a set face and climbed feet first into the trunk. When the hatch was closed and a baptismal shower of lukewarm water sprayed her head, she let go and pressed elbows and knees into the smooth slime of the sides to slow the fall.

It was not bad at all as an experience. The conduit made several gradual turns to pick up from other disposal points. Except for throat-catching stench, it was even agreeable, like falling out of the world down a deep well of unknowing.

Eyes closed, she felt the change of direction for the last pitch and then a change in texture as she skidded out into a slow-moving conveyer trough. Bedall's caution about the destructor at the end of the line made her sit up and grab for the sides.

It was still semidark and her sense of direction was all to hell. But there were dim figures moving about beside the line.

Pamela Harte struggled to her feet and took a hand courteously held out to help her over the top.

It was a firm grip, well suited for the chore, but metal cold. Belatedly, she tried to struggle free as she was passed over to another standing farther back and acting as tally clerk for the enterprise. This one shot a measured dose of serum point blank into her chest and said with every satisfaction. "Number Ten. Two more to come."

CHAPTER NINE

Roger Diment left his car in a municipal parking lot outside city limits and went on foot in the mild afternoon sunshine on a zigzag route across the high spidery walkways that lay like metallic tape over the town.

There was no challenge. The special agents seemed to have been withdrawn, and the local security force was doing its own thing out of the public gaze. Fresh from the country, he was seeing the city with a new eye. It was too big; too impersonal for the human mind to get a comprehensive grip on it.

Men were more comfortable in a village.

Bedall had created a village at that. Also, thinking back, he had virtually created his own village in the weaponry complex. That was the whole point of shibboleths in all times: accents, group vocabulary, dress, manners, and customs. The full spectrum was too big. Isolate a small range that the mind could grapple with. Maybe Government with a big G had foundered on that small fact. When it was found to be too difficult to legislate for the millions, retreat from maturity as an ideal had set in.

Pamela Harte would be interested in the theory.

And Bedall. He quickened his pace unconsciously, anxious for a homecoming in a way he had not been before.

A block away from the museum complex, he slowed again. It shouldn't be this easy. Also, there was something wrong with the city. He had never known it so quiet in an afternoon when everybody, having done their simple stint in the morning session, had the freedom of the marketplace.

As he rounded the last corner, it was all made plain. The plateau and its surrounds were packed with people, and a cordon of regular security guards was lined up shoulder to shoulder to keep an apron clear in front of the museum porch.

It was a silent crowd, motionless, eyes fixed on the double doors that opened abruptly for two silver androids to whip out and stand on either side.

Then a third appeared holding a cord, followed by a bead chain of twelve variously dressed like tribal representatives in a Roman triumph.

The cord was looped at neck level so that any faltering by one would be felt by all and they kept in step moving smartly down the short, broad flight of stairs toward two cars waiting on the level.

Pamela Harte was number ten on the string, recognizable by her ringlet and her walk.

Three more androids followed the column out and one walked quickly up the line and cut the rope after number six. Then half the catch was bundled into either car.

Somebody in the dense crowd began to hiss and it was taken up. At some deep level, it had been understood that the bell was tolling for more than twelve.

The noise gathered like a long pent-up escape of a vast head of steam. There had been no demonstration of the kind in living memory. The guards drew riot sticks and prepared to beat into the front rank. But there was no movement forward.

The cars lifted in vertical takeoff. Hovered. Turned slowly for orientation and accelerated away. The hissing cut off. Patently, whatever it was, was all over. As if on a signal, they began to disperse, and Diment mingled with the homeward scatter, temporarily out of program.

There was a definite air of unease. Rumor painted full of tongues was having a field day. But they could make nothing of it. Complacency ran deep. He reckoned that by the morning they would be back in the groove. And as far as all the other teeming cities of the Western Federation were concerned, there had not been even this surface scratch on the body politic.

When he finally reached his car, he sat looking through the windshield with unseeing eyes until light levels began to fall.

Color, seeping through the plexiglass dome at his back, dyed his hands red. The parking lot was on rising ground overlooking the sea. When he slewed round in his seat he saw that the sun was standing like a blood-red penny on the horizon. The bay was a lake of molten fire and the sky was dividing its canvas in broad bands of cadmium yellow and vermilion.

Dramatic sunsets were a feature of the coast. He had seen it often enough. But he could have been looking at it for the first time. It shook him like a blare of brass and the combined entry of every percussion instrument on the platform.

He said illogically, "The bastards. The bastards," and began to swear in a monotone.

Nonproductive thinking though it was, it brought

him into action. Decision crystallized somewhere in
the subconscious heap and he shifted round again
to the console.

Horace Johnson's shuttle lifted in a crash climb
and he swung on to Freeway Six with the motor in
a howl.

Traffic Control, picking up the movement, called
urgently, "Reduce speed. Declare identity."

Diment, who had definitively crossed every spiri-
tual and emotional Rubicon, went over to transmit
at full power and snarled into the grille, "Stuff yourself up your little tin ass."

Ten minutes later, he was circling the control
tower of Regional Farm Seven, bitterly certain that
every patrol car in the area would be closing in to
pick him up.

The apron was empty. Miss Raidney had gone
and he had a shrewd idea where she was heading.
The tiller combine had been retracted to its starting
point, and in the last of the light he could see that
only the first fifty meters of the strip had been given
the shock treatment.

He dropped the car on its skids close to the porch.
Still tied in some respects to nature's own rhythm,
the farming staff had closed for the night. A carefully rationed blast cooked the lock. He crossed to
the elevator with the phasor ready to make a last
contribution and was in the cage without challenge,
thumbing the selector for the freight dispatch
level.

Out on the landing, he was less sure that he would
find what he was looking for. The marshaling yard
confined underground seemed bigger in surface area
than the farm itself. Maybe anyway it was a bulk
breaking point for produce from other parts of the
region. Brilliantly lit, it stretched away into distance

until the roof joined the floor in a bright blur. There was a succession of parallel bays and platforms stacked with barrels, crates, carboys, packing cases of every shape and size, and a constant weaving run of fork lift trucks driven by remote control from a control kiosk in the center of every site.

Whatever else it failed on, the system had gotten the logistics of feeding the cities all buttoned up.

Diment stood still to sort it out and the cage at his back began to lift. There was not much time. The gendarmes were closing in.

Reason said that the Organizers would have their private line close to the tower core. He tried left, along the landing he was on and came to a dead end. Only storage bays that way. As he passed the elevator, working along for the other side, he saw its indicator flicking along. They were almost down.

The third archway was the payoff. It opened onto a small platform with a single monorail car. Heavy feet were pounding along the landing as he slid back its forward hatch and hauled himself inside.

It was no freight carrier. Very plushy with a tasteful decor in pastel shades and deep upholstery, acceptable even to a tin can. The operating console was set for auto, but there was a dual spread for a local pilot. More to the point, there was a route diagram showing where the line had intersections with other tunnels. Its terminus was marked URANIA CITY.

Switchgear was near enough after the pattern of a regular shuttle, and the car moved off with a smooth surge of power that settled him back into his well-sprung seat.

He was a hundred meters down the tube, with a searchlight beam probing ahead from a point above the windshield, before the first guard reached the archway, looked down the empty platform, registered a negative, and motivated itself to carry on up the creek.

The monocar hit its ceiling at a hundred and fifty kilometers in the hour. On its console a bright dot moved slowly over the route diagram to show its position on the circuit. Diment reckoned that less than half an hour would see him underneath Urania City.

In that, he was some hours behind the twelve burghers of Barnston. They were already settled in.

Having no criminal classes of their own, the Organizers were short on detention facilities. Instead, they were using a six-berth ward in the city medicenter wired for sound and vision, so that no aseptic corner was out of range of a viewing monitor.

The arrivals had been screened for alien contamination, stripped, power washed, air-dried, and issued with a plain white unisex gown without even a cord to stop any disinfected draught having free run from hem to halter.

Not that there were any. The air was still, redolent of iodoform. A clock thermometer on the wall was reading a steady twenty Celsius.

Pamela Harte and Carol Greer, sitting together on one trundle bed, had not spoken for a good ten minutes. The atmosphere had finally gotten through to where they lived. It was a sterile limbo, an anteroom to dissolution.

Williams, who had been pacing about in his smock, stopped beside Roy Stanwick at the closed hatch and asked the question which was hanging about, only waiting for a form of words. "What's their angle, Roy? What do you reckon they brought us here for?"

"Observation, questioning. Replacements on the hoof for that transplant unit we came through."

"They've surely got all they need to keep that going. Harry Bedall would have liked to see that. It always bothers him to know what they do with all the spare parts."

Pamela Harte said, "Bothered."

"What's that Pamela?"

"I said 'bothered.' Past tense. I didn't tell you at the time; but when I was waiting for my turn on the chute, I slipped up top to see what was going on. Those silver gribbles lined them all up and killed them."

It was a monstrous fact, but in their curious, dreamlike suspension of ordinary living, they accepted it as truth and could not react to the pity of it.

Carol Greer shied off altogether on a different tack. "I still don't understand this transplant bit. What do androids want with human organs and human blood? They're giving themselves problems they don't need to have."

It triggered a Cassandra-like statement from her bedfellow. Pamela Harte, building on a knowledge of android assembly and making a leap in understanding by some sudden intuition, said slowly, "I've been thinking about that. It's the last stage of android development. Man tried for centuries to build a model like himself. He could copy everything —body shell, moving limbs, a brain with as many unit cells as his own, the whole cognitive apparatus. But he couldn't manage the orectic side—the feeling and striving, the whole emotional bag of tricks that came from body tone. Viscera come into it. Emotion moves like a shifting electric field through the brain and turns a biological machine into a person. When the androids started making themselves, they saw what was missing. They've turned themselves into people."

The Chief Organizer, watching on a screen in her executive suite, said to Yolanda Raidney, "That one is very clever. Which is surprising when you read her profile card. There is no evidence that she was anything but a normal immature sensation-seeker up to the Wayfarer stage. She has developed a strong cognitive side in a short time. It might be interesting to keep her alive. But she is the one you are interested in. I should be jealous about that. Except that your intentions are strictly destructive and she will not be with us long. Also, the girl has not got it quite right. We have succeeded in building human-type emotion into our psyche, but only for pleasure. It is always kept in its place."

The people's choice, unconscious of attention in high places, was going on with her analysis of the scene as she saw it. "Mind you, they're not as clever as they think they are. They couldn't have set it up without a few lucky breaks. It was a failure of nerve on our part more than a direct confrontation. We left a power vacuum and they gradually sidled into it."

It had the ring of truth. Roy Stanwick said, "Very likely. It's great to get it straight. But it doesn't help us as of now. What do the mechanical marvels want with us here?"

Williams could have said that he had already asked for clarification on that point. There was still no answer from the group. But a voice spoke from the center of the room as if by a ventriloquist's trick. "The woman Pamela Harte is to go to the door. It is open. Nobody else is to try to get out."

Carol Greer said, "Don't go. We're in this together. We won't let them take you." At the same time she put one arm round her shoulders.

Pamela Harte shook it off and stood up. She said shakily, "We can't stop them. Thank you anyway. If it isn't now it will be later. If it isn't later it will be now." She walked firmly over to the hatch. It was all true. It slid away at a touch. Outside, a silver android was waiting. It turned on its heel and moved off expecting to be followed.

The door closed behind her with a definitive click.

Roger Diment slowed the monocar to a crawl and paid out a cord looped over the rheostat lever that controlled forward speed, until he was balanced on the threshold of the open entry port, with a sack of useful gear in his left hand. From various lockers in the car, he had found two fully charged phasors, a vibrator pack, and a large self-energizing torch. He looked down at the narrow space beside the moving car and rehearsed the sequence. Pitch out sack. Jump. Pull cord. Gauging it to match the forward speed, he launched himself out at a backward slant, heaving on the cord as his feet left the deck.

Then he was fending off the smooth tunnel wall with both hands and falling back toward the track. He was heavily loaded with a selection of phasors.

The car whipped away as if booted up its rumble. He hit the monorail only centimeters behind its hurrying bullet back.

The sack was farther down the line than he expected and he found it by falling over it when he thought he must have missed it in the pitch dark.

He fished out the torch and used it to empty the rest, sticking the two phasors into his waistband and settling the vibrator pack on his back.

The car had disappeared ahead round a slow

curve and would be already running below the city. According to the diagram, it would pass two subsidiary stations before it ran into the main terminal.

On the chart it had not seemed far, but he was ten minutes before there was growing light ahead and he rounded a gradual left hand curve to see the tunnel funneling out into a large, circular hall with a criss-cross of platform escalators dropping like stalactites from the cave roof, and other monorails coming in like spokes to a hub.

There were three stationary cars, one at nine o'clock on the circle, hatches open, waiting for its quota of commuters. Two at one o'clock, on the same track, coupled together and in process of being loaded from a stack of stores. There were androids about on every platform, having no labor union to protect them from excessive wear and tear or claim double time for the dogwatch. But no silver specials in open view.

Diment walked out along the track, heaved himself onto the first platform, and stood with a phasor in either hand waiting for a reaction.

There was none. He walked deliberately to the nearest escalator and might have been a regular traveler on the line. As his weight came on the first step it started up and carried him on at a smart walking pace to a broad landing which gave him a selection of three more.

One was labeled *IBT Terminal*; another *Polyxo Suburb*; the third *Industrial Precinct*. Not a choice to have a man hopping excitedly from one foot to the other.

Pamela would not be held in a suburb. Nor would the group be shipped out on an Intercontinental Ballistic Transporter. The Industrial Precinct was a negative winner and might offer an ongoing route which would be less obvious to any reception party which had been set up.

The noise from the landing when he reached the area in two long doglegs on the escalator was enough to camouflage any activity whatever.

Since no human operators were in the sector, they had solved the industrial fatigue bit by disconnecting aural sensors in the work force.

Skirting the fringe of an assembly line for plug-in housing units, Diment reckoned that half an hour on the site would unhinge the mind. An enormous robot figure, nudging the three-meter mark and broad in proportion was emptying heavy molds by lifting them with one massive fist and pounding them on the bottom with the other. A one-hundred-kilogram slab dropped with an earthquake thud into a solid-wheeled tumbril which whipped it off for the next process.

As the industrial colossus turned round to pick up another mold, there was a visual shock to match the decibel battery. Like Max Ernst's *Saint Cecilia,* there was an incongruous element inside the monster shell. A regular, general-purpose android was standing inside the stakhanovite worker with its arms and legs in the hollow limbs, and its movements were amplified and given megapower by the superstructure.

As far as Diment could see, there were no controls. It was a straight case of movement being picked up from the android circuits and fed to mechanical muscles.

He edged cautiously up to the workhead and waited for the power suit to make another trip. As it turned he fell in step close behind and considered the angles. There was no doubt, the inner unit was detachable.

Using a phasor at point blank range he shot a minute charge into its cortex.

The composite figure stopped dead, one elephantine leg poised for a stride.

Diment plucked the android operator from its nest and dumped it on the next waiting carrier. Then he stepped into the empty case.

First moves almost brought disaster. In spite of the mass of metal, there was no sensation of weight. It was like walking without gravity. Magnified by super power, his first two strides took him through a plexiglass screen into a whirling white cloud where fine clay was being processed for ceramics.

Direction clouded and semistupified by the overall din, he cut a swathe through a stack of unglazed lavatory fixtures before he made out through another party wall into a fiber glass panel plant.

A white, apocalyptic figure, he would have ruined any shop steward's midshift tea break, but the resident labor force soldiered on without a second look. Now he had gotten the hang of it and moved neatly down a circulation alley to an outer exit.

Fine manipulation was still tricky. The two-leaf door came away in his hands and he lumbered into the corridor with the two sections flapping like demented wings before he could shake them off.

A silver android, putting in a routine inspection tour of the complex, stood still, busily searching its memory banks for a suitable program. Fast as it was in coming up with the view that it was facing a case of public disorder, it was not quick enough.

A massive hand slapped onto its chest and ran it two paces back to the nearest wall, then the other dropped over its frantically turning visual sensor, closed to a grinding grip, and began to screw off its head.

It was a weakness in design that had not seemed important to its creators. They had reckoned that nothing would get near enough to a special android to find out.

Diment shook the head like an ape testing a coconut and pitched it over his shoulder, partly for luck and partly to practice fine control. It shot through the empty door frame like a silver cannon ball, carving a way through three partitions before it dropped, all passion spent, in a heap of concrete mix ready to be poured into a mold. Self-energizing, its brain unit would go on working out the angles for years to come, the only thinking wall of the age.

Diment, gaining expertise every minute, backtracked to the landing and took a fresh direction, this time for the IBT Terminal.

The escalator head was central in a large hexagonal crush hall with an information kiosk close by and destination indicators dotted about. A few Organizers were sitting on long settles drinking coffee for the pleasure of it. They were all dressed in normal rig, ready to take their place in other cities in the Federation. But Diment, with a kind of ESP working for him, could recognize the genre.

A pedestal-bound android in the kiosk saw Diment's monstrous shadow fall over the desk and spun round to see what was o'clock. Without having to think, it recognized that what it saw constituted a breach of the peace and grabbed for an alarm pull overhead.

It was a brave gesture. Diment's hand was interposed like a new instant ceiling. Taxing his newfound skill to the limit, he took both the android's arms and tied them in a neat knot under its notional chin. Then he balled one fist and clubbed it on its dome.

The action had not gone unnoticed. Organizers started from their seats. One dropped his coffee cup and the small crash was a signal for Diment to speak. He had withdrawn one arm from its shell and poked a phasor from a pop hole in the chest cavity. He said, "Hold it there. Everybody step this way. I'll have you all together in a friendly group."

One was near enough the porch to try a break. He had his hand on the latch when Diment picked up the contrary movement. He shot once and a number of questions were answered. For a split second the external metallic form of the super android was irradiated and clear to see, with its quota of human organs visible as if on an X-ray plate.

For Diment, the last piece of the jigsaw dropped into place. He knew for a truth where the surplus human organs found their journey's end. It added a convincing bite to his voice as he said, "Believe me, I only want half a reason to do that all round. Move along."

He collected seven. Three female variants and four male. All anxious to oblige. The search for human qualities had its drawback. Unlike other androids, they could feel fear and a basic self-interest, which put personal survival high on the motivation list.

Driving his hostages ahead in a bunch, he went out onto the porch and looked around the terminal.

There were six long-distance passenger rockets on the pads, two being serviced by fuel tenders. Over right, a kilometer distant, there was a closed-off area and a close-packed array of larger rocket ships all painted steel gray. Close beside it was an entrance for ground traffic with a large sign which he could read backward as URANIA CITY SPACEPORT.

He picked up the nearest Organizer by the slack of his tunic and gave him a preliminary shake to get his ideas in order. "What are those ships over there?"

"Those are not used. They are military craft. Since we have abolished war, they are not needed."

"But they work?"

"I believe they are regularly maintained and kept at instant readiness. But they have nuclear warheads which could be armed in an emergency."

"We'll take a look."

A toast-rack, six-wheeled trolley stood on the apron to take passengers out to their craft. He shepherded his seven into the front seats, with the knowledgeable one in the driving seat and broke out one row to give room for his bulk. Then he said, "Action, action. Drive over to the military pen."

A long peace and a sure belief that there was nothing left to threaten their hold on the system had led to a slackening of security measures at the pen. There was no guard at the barrier when Diment said, "Don't anybody move," and lumbered out to take the red check pole in a double grip and tear it from its hoisting gear. Then he beckoned the car through and walked beside it with one hand on the hood.

Close up, the rockets dwarfed even his new King Kong persona. Each was ready mounted on a tracked facility vehicle, which could move it out to a launch site in the airport. But then, with the germ of an idea kindling in his mind, he reckoned he would only need one and the damage done to the rest by a blastoff in confined quarters was not his worry.

He stopped at the nearest, a slim minaret with the reference XX9 in meter-high lettering on each of its three stabilizers. There was a tangible increase in heat levels and a shimmer in the air. The Organizer was truth its own self. It was kept ready for blast off.

The suit was too clumsy and he stepped out of it, shoving the spare phasor in his belt, humping the vibrator gear, and motioning the pilot to back off.

It was a calculated risk, but he reckoned it would be a few minutes before one of them realized that opportunity had knocked.

He climbed a built-in iron ladder to the launch platform and saw that massive clips had dropped over to engage on lugs in each stabilizer. That could only be cleared by remote control, so he unshipped the vibrator and sliced through the shank.

It took four minutes and a siren wail started up from the Control Tower. His own party had not moved and were sitting looking up at the gantry like a school tour.

He walked round the base looking up. It was clear all the way except at one point where the gangway into the main hatch appeared to engage on a locking bar in the rocket shell.

He sent a phasor shot to shatter the parquet in front of the car as a reminder and raced for a power ladder that ran up the inside of the gantry. Drive was on, and as soon as his weight hit the rungs they began to lift.

From the gangway he could see all over the port, and a collection of tenders, shuttles, and riot cars was weaving out from behind the control tower.

Diment, working like a robot, tested the hatch, found it opened to a touch, and sliced a meter gap from its coaming along the gangplank.

Then as the piece went into free fall, he was racing down to his toast rack.

The gift of emotion was again proved to bring its share of pain. None of the passengers looked pleased to see him. They had reckoned that he had intended to take off in solo flight out of their lives.

Disappointment colored the pilot's tone as he asked, "What now?"

Diment said, "Where would your special guards take a group of prisoners?"

One of the females, who had been acting up as though rank entitled her to better treatment, said tartly, "How should we know that? That is not our business."

Diment, once more in his power suit, stretched over a grab and cuffed her on the side of her well-coiffured head.

"Who would know?"

Sulky but prompt, she said, "Only the Chief Organizer."

"Where does he live?"

"*She* lives in the admin silo in the central square."

"That's our destination. Move it along, pilot, before your friends find you fried like any egg."

The driver did his best and the toast rack whipped through the shattered gate with its small wheels in a speed slip.

The posse, halfway across the apron, saw the move and began to veer over, but they were too far off to intercept. Diment had lifted a portcullis off its guides and thrown it on the roof of the gatehouse when they were still three hundred meters off.

Outside, they were in the metropolitan throughway, which linked the main sectors of the city and bounced along at the car's ceiling speed of sixty kilometers in the hour.

They skidded to a halt at the admin silo porch still ahead of the field.

A round dozen special androids were lined up along the frontage and Diment knew that mechanical power would not be enough. One or more would get in a phasor beam to boil him in his shell.

He leaned forward from his seat, scooped in two Organizers, and stood up with one in each arm.

He said, "Now we can find out what value you put on survival. Tell those zombies to stand aside and let me pass."

There was no need to add that any fancy shooting would get to them first. It was obvious to the female on his left arm, who had crossed him before. She called out, "I am Controller Dolan. Do as he says."

Diment stepped out of the car and walked up the porch, conscious from noise in the square that an all-services contingent was pulling in behind him.

The two silver androids dead ahead moved slowly aside, clearly dubious whether the Controller should be obeyed or not.

Through the glass, Diment could see that the reception area was empty and, he went through backward in case his unprotected rear should trigger off a change of heart.

For a count of three he was cut off in cloistered calm as the closing doors put on an acoustic seal. Then the reception area vibrated with an amplified scream, stereo-engineered so that the screamer could have been standing on his left foot.

It had a familiar ring and he had identified it before the Chief Organizer's voice said coldly, "That was your companion, the female known as Pamela Harte. Stand away from your power suit and throw your phasor weapons toward the door. Otherwise she will suffer great pain."

Additional evidence that it was true came from the victim herself. Speaking very quickly in a strained whisper, Pamela Harte said, "Don't do it Roger. Kill all the . . . ." She was not quick enough. Speech trailed off in a whimper of protest that had nothing human in it before it escalated into another frantic, heart-stopping cry.

CHAPTER TEN

Diment had pitched the male Organizer away and was making metallic scrap of the elevator gate with his free hand when the screaming cut off. In the following silence his voice boomed up the trunk.

"Okay. You've made your point. What do I have to do?"

Continuous sobbing made a carrier wave for the Chief Organizer to say, "Do not waste my time. You know what I said. Do it."

"How do I know that you will not kill her anyway?"

"You don't know. But the contrary is sure."

"I have one of your Controllers here. Send her down and you can have this one in exchange. Otherwise I'll take it apart."

"You miss an important difference between us. Our hostage is expendable, yours is not. That is no equal trade. You will have to decide what value you put on your friend. The human brain is supposedly quicker than the fastest electronic computer. You have ten seconds to arrive at a decision."

Diment took nine. It was a lifetime in miniature with the human idea through the millennia presented in a vast tableau to his mind's eye. At every stage, institutionalized man had set up an apparatus of government and social organization which had finally overwhelmed him. Once his simple village ethos had been stretched beyond a certain point it had become too thin a container for all the clap-trap sociopolitical rubble that had been shoveled into it. Then the strain was too great and it broke down and the institution, whatever it was, careered on under its own dynamic, on a course that no-body in their right mind would want.

Until this last. Stability in the end had come when the human race had handed itself over to outside direction. Family group gone; democratic rights gone; biological rights gone; the sense of right that had needled man like a built-in goad on his illusionary treadmill of progress, finally gone or stilled at last by a regular diet of euphorics.

It had left the pleasure-pain principle as the one true motivator. The hedonists had found their final vindication. A simple brief life of the senses had become the norm.

But it was not enough. The life force, identified in the last analysis with the truth that there was more to man than a belly and a phallus, would not be denied for ever.

There would be others after him. Like Harry Bedall and Carl Borsey. He was not the one and only torchbearer.

That left him with a gesture. There was an out-side chance that he could make it alone in the power suit to the rocket park and get away for an extension of his personal span. But that would put him on the same footing as the Organizers. Loyalty to a person was the one human trait he had left.

The fact that it was Pamela Harte with her dark

ringlet and unique three-mole cluster was important, but not the deciding factor. He would have to do it if it had been Gribbin up there in the Chief Organizer's pad.

He released the Organizer still clutched in the power suit's left arm and shoved her away. Then he stepped out of the body shell and pitched the two phasors on the deck at its feet.

The Chief Organizer's voice said, "An interesting decision. You may come up to my office."

He heard the same voice filtered through the glass screen speaking outside to the crowd. "The emergency is over. Return to your stations."

On the top landing, two silver androids fell in beside him to conduct him through the tropical garden belt to the hub.

At first, he missed Pamela Harte on the crowded, opulent set. There was a heavy pollen cloud from the high command, compounded of geranium and verbena. Although there was enough daylight for any normal use coming in from a panoramic window spread, there was a lot of top lighting and a whole battery of spots concentrating on a silver android who stood just off center with his arms outstretched and feet astride.

A second silver android stood inside the door and took over as the two escorts wheeled away, duty done. He followed Diment, a pace in the rear, into the working area.

The top brass stood together like a singing sister duo in identical crotch-length tabards of deep apricot hue.

For a power combine that dominated more of the world than any ancient empire had ever dreamed about, it was a gratuitous insult to Clio her own self and to the dumb masses of those currently being manipulated. It was like finding a soft, obscene jelly at the center of a rock.

Diment grated out, "Where is she?"

He missed Yolanda Raidney's nod to the illuminated android but he saw the man swivel cleverly on one foot to face him.

Pamela Harte was neatly staked out on the cross he was making. Feet on his feet, ankles held by strips of fancy fabric. Wrists on his forearms. Skin blotched by small angry red areas. Head slumped forward with her dark ringlet in free fall.

It was a credit to the Personnel Adviser's flair for improvisation, and she was clearly looking pleased about it, with her red tongue permanently moving over her upper lip.

The smiling face tipped Diment over the edge. The scene dissolved in a red haze, then cleared with every detail luminously clear and hard-edged as though he was seeing the material world for the first time.

Perceptions sharpened so that he could visualize the movement of the android behind him. He quickened his step, as though making for the Chief Organizer, then checked abruptly and dropped on one knee.

It was fair proof of her thesis about the human brain being quicker off the mark. As its data acquisition network registered the new information it was already too late to check its forward movement.

Diment grabbed sure and true and brought it over his bent back in a throw that scattered the two Organizers.

Then he went coldly and destructively mad.

Before the android had hit the parquet, with its gyro stabilizers fighting a losing rearguard, Diment

had launched himself from his crouch in a shallow
dive that brought him sliding over the metal torso.

Every action was crystal clear, with no hangups
waiting for a program. Recall of his last experience
with a silver android was pasted up like a working
diagram, including a correction for the fact that this
one was in reverse. His hands locked on the head
as it touched down. If he had had to go by trial
and error he would have been seconds too late. The
android was beginning to turn when its head completed the contrary cycle that sprang a locking clip.

Diment rose to his feet with the head in two
hands like a football player looking for a gap in the
defense.

The Chief Organizer reckoned it was time to
release her second guard from its crucifixion stint.
Her mouth was open to give the good word that
would restore it to independent action, though any
move it made would dislocate its white albatross.

Diment, with a kind of E.S.P. working for him,
pitched the head at less than three meters range in
a hard, true throw that hit her between the eyes and
literally stopped her dead in her tracks.

Her hands had moved automatically to protect
her face and caught the silver ovoid as it fell. Beyond a shallow dent between the arched eyebrows
there was no visible damage done, but the hammer
blow had shaken some vital contact out of circuit.

Kohl-rimmed eyes were opening and closing, one
at a time in a lascivious wink, long lashes beating
like silky fans. But it was her only contribution.

Yolanda Raidney, still full of sap and brio, had
come to the view that more androids on the set
could only be good. Still relatively unfamiliar with
all the refined control gear in the apartment, she
judged it would be quicker to take a personal mes-

sage. She was two meters from the hatch and moving well for one who had seen a close friend struck down, when Diment leapt the back of the settle like a hurdler and carried her with him by unstoppable momentum to fetch up with her back flat against the wall.

At close quarters, it was clear that she had been responsible for the verbena element in the scent symphony. Crushing her flat, with his forearm lodged across her throat, it was also easy to understand why Bedall's grip on the difference between android and human had gotten blurred.

This one was a lot farther along the line than Amenophis's daughter. Body texture was on the firm side, but pneumatic enough, skin was flawless, hair, brushing his cheek, was fine silk.

But the eyes gave the game away. In spite of the action they were cold, calculating, mechanical sensors, open now at full stretch to estimate what he would do.

It was an easy decision. Diment shifted his arm from her throat and sited it behind her shoulders. Then he put the heel of his free hand under her chin and pushed, muscle cording along his back.

He went on until he was holding up a dead weight. Then he carried her to the settle and draped her over one end to flash her neat jasmine briefs at her winking overlord.

Returning to her closed circuit of pain, with a shuddering intake of breath, Pamela Harte had every reason to believe that she had slipped back in time to the closing stages of a Wayfarer party.

The only movement was behind her and, hazily trying to check it out, she found she could not move hand or foot. Total recall flooded in, and it was all bad.

With the method established as a craft skill, Diment collected his third android head and parked it on a half-meter crystal cube, which was earning its place in the decor by flushing continuously with a kaleidoscopic pattern of colored shapes.

Then he went round to see how Pamela was getting on.

For her part, she thought it was a last vision come to torment the final phase of her exit from the world of sense. She said uncertainly, "Roger. Roger Diment," as though adding the full label would prove it one way or another.

Before admitting that it was none other, he freed her ankles, then her wrists, taking that order on the principle that when springing a trap, it was only prudent to watch that the victim did not take a piece out of the do-gooder in simple reaction.

It was an unnecessary precaution. As her arms came free, she put them round his neck as if carrying on from the point where Horace Johnson had leaned over her bed.

There was no longer any reasonable area of doubt. He was there, present in the flesh, seemingly under Trappist vows and slippery with sweat after his concentrated output of work done, but on all counts the same. She said "Roger" again as a statement of fact, and followed it by a gasp as his arms went round her in a bear hug.

Roger Diment said anxiously, "Are you all right?"

"That's a relative question. I'm sore everywhere a girl can be. But I don't think there's been any permanent damage done, yet."

Reaction started a muscular tremble which even his comprehensive grip could not damp down.

"You need something on."

Yolanda Raidney was a natural for losing her

tabard, and he drew it over her head without disturbing her position.

He would have gone further in a good cause, but he was stopped. "Don't bother. This'll be fine. Are we going far?"

Diment was roaming round the pad looking for a second exit. There was a trick door opening on to the roof, which was laid out in Chinese style with carefully engineered prospects, a bridge over a stream, and even a miniature mountain.

Beyond a low hedge was the shining plexiglass dome of the chief citizen's personal car.

They were crossing the bridge hand in hand, hurrying lovers in a Willow Pattern, when Pamela Harte stood still.

"What is it?"

"The others. We can't leave the others."

"Where are they?"

"In a medicenter. Not far. Two or three minutes' walk through a subway."

"It's pushing our luck."

"If we don't do it, we don't deserve any luck."

Diment looked at her. Nobody could have blamed her if she had opted for out at any price; but she was prepared to put herself back in baulk.

ESP working strongly, she said, "Believe me, I'd rather not, but we couldn't ever forget it, could we, if we didn't even try?"

"You're a great girl, Pamela. A real person. And there aren't many about. Maybe never have been. Okay. How do I get there?"

"You wouldn't leave me here?"

"All right, there's no time for a big argument. Sooner or later somebody's going to try to contact the big white chief and will want more answer than a lewd wink. Lead on."

"What about the androids in the anteroom?"

"That's it. Send them off to bring up the rest of the party."

They were back in the executive suite when Pamela Harte put her finger on the serious flaw. "But they never leave the landing. It was a different one that brought me along."

Diment was checking over an elaborate communications console. Four small subpanels labeled *Personal Security* were also numbered with the X series carried by special androids. Two numbers matched the two headless trunks in the room. It was a fair bet that the other two were the outside staff.

He said, "Try to copy the Chief Organizer's voice. When I switch over, call X0017 and X0016. Just say, This cancels any fixed program. Go to the medicenter and bring along the remainder of the human party—anyway, you know the jargon. You worked on these gribbles, didn't you?"

"Not these, but an android is an android. Remind me about that later. I have some deep thoughts about that."

"When I picked you off that conveyer for your three moles, I didn't know what a needle brain I was getting at the other end."

Gratitude had not turned her into a cipher. She said, "Quiet. God alone he knows how you've survived so long."

Her change of voice when she began to speak had him looking at the still figure of the Chief Organizer. A good mimic had been lost to the vaudeville stage. There was only a momentary hesitation as relays tripped to override the permanent element of the program. Then the responses came back in numerical order.

"X0016. Check. I am leaving now."

"X0017. Check. I am leaving now."

Diment followed their progress on the scanner which must have been used to monitor his own progress in the hall below. When they were clear, he said, "There's a very useful piece of equipment down there. I'll go and get it."

Before she could file any objection he was out into the shrubbery.

Left alone, Pamela Harte checked the rooms. The boudoir was missing a regular bed as being unnecessary for an unsleeping android. It had a circular upholstered play area with loose cushions, set in a shallow well and three broad stairs leading into it.

She found an amphora of skin cream heavily scented with sandalwood, slipped out of her tabard, and did a cautious massage job. By the time she heard the outer hatch slide open to signal Diment's return, she had snapped into a gauzy equalizer with a neat rosebud motif, ultrasheer snowflake tights, gold sandals, and a filigree electrum thread tabard. She was feeling ahead of the game and came through with a light step and her usual "Roger," spoken this time as delighted welcome, expecting an answer compounded of awe and admiration.

Roger Diment had stooped to get the power suit through the door and straightened to its full commanding height once over the threshold.

If she could have seen his face, she would have been reassured, but the functional mask of the power suit was a black stranger. Even his voice, baffled by the heavy grooving, was unfamiliar.

Pat on cue, he said, "It is my lady. O it is my love."

Menace set the key and like a textbook Gestalt illustration, her startled sensors, confused by the rigors of the day, made a logical pattern of it. She heard, "It is too late. Hold still and do not move."

She shot back to the boudoir like a shiny rabbit.

Diment climbed out of his suit and followed at a run. They had gone twice round the playpen with Pamela holding a five-meter lead, when Carol Greer spoke from the archway, "What kind of bedroom game is that?"

Diment stopped dead, bitterly condemning himself for being sidetracked from the main issue. If the prisoners were in, the outside guards must have taken a good look into the room.

Before anybody could answer the reasonable question, the frantic wail of a siren started up from the roof.

The androids had done the sum, but were stuck with the program that they could not enter the excutive suite without a direct instruction from a superior. As a next best line of action, they had pulled the plug for a general alarm.

They crossed the garden in a bizzarre file; eleven in white shapeless gowns. Pamela Harte reflecting the late afternoon sun in a continuous shimmer and the black power suit, in the van, as a grotesque Pied Piper.

Every hexagonal tower in Urania City was sending out an iron-tongued clamor. Every Organizer and special guard was being paged with a three-line whip. The state was in danger.

It was a tight squeeze to get the full company embused in the executive black and gold shuttle. Carol Greer said it reminded her of an ancient film sequence from the archives and she reckoned they must have done it by going through a hole in the deck.

Williams had picked up a phasor and was standing on her lap, head and shoulders through a pop hole in the dome. He called through urgently, "Here they come. For godsake move it along."

A dozen silver androids had fanned out from the penthouse, running in a half circle to surround the car.

Its console had registered overweight, and Diment was searching for a trip to override the circuit breaker.

When he found it, the nearest android was ten meters off with a clear target raising its arm to fire.

Williams hit it full in the chest, too late to halt the sequence its computer had set. As the car rose, it fired and an incandescent beam lanced out to melt away the nearside landing skid.

Clear of the tower, they could see frenetic activity in the streets. Urania City had turned into a disturbed termite hill. Cars were taking off from every landing strip. Surface shuttles were offloading squads of special androids on the apron in front of the executive silo. Organizers were gathering in the squares and on the walkways.

Roy Stanwick, crushed on the squab beside the pilot, said, "We won't make the city limits."

Diment was totally concentrated. From the tail of his eye he saw the glittering shape of a security shuttle coming out of the sun behind him. It had gained height in a vertical lift and was coming in with a built-in phasor throwing a brilliant rope from between its landing skids. He slammed every control into a dead stop and and gravity plucked them down like a stone.

There was a plosive crack and the crowded cabin filled with hot shards of plexiglass as the dome disintegrated. But the car was past in a wow of power and Diment opened up again.

Before it could pull out of its dive, Williams, with blood streaming from his head and his hair singed to an instant tonsure, had fired into its withdrawing stern. Its motor cut and as Diment brought them round on a new course, they saw its nose dip away.

From two blocks away, they heard the crash and saw the column of smoke and flame mushroom up.

Diment was piloting a visual course. He could see the cluster of spires that marked the I.B.T. Terminal. He had flogged the wreck to its ceiling speed and the airflow was doing its best to pluck his crew from their seats.

He went in over a rooftop in a shallow dive, banked steeply, so that Pamela Harte's ringlet was pointing like a dark finger at the pad and came to a crash landing twenty meters from the massive facility vehicle that held the military rocket.

Watchers from the control tower had seen the move. Tenders were racing out before the wreck had stopped bouncing on its remaining hydraulic skid. Cars from every quarter of the city were landing on every part of the strip, baulked from a direct touchdown in the military pen by the clutter of gear and the close-packed rocket ships themselves.

Diment drove them. A solid ring of silver androids was closing in at a steady run.

He stood on the narrow platform of the gantry in the power suit, plucking each one from the rungs of the ladder and fairly throwing them along the gangplank to the open hatch of XX9.

As Roy Stanwick, climbing last, made the passage, Diment leaned down and tore the last two meters of ladder free from its clips and dropped it onto the android climbing ten meters below. Then he shuffled out, feeling the catwalk sag under his weight.

Inside, they were all packed together in the reception bay. As he stepped out of the suit, Williams said, "We couldn't have gone far. But is this good? They'll cut through that hatch in seconds with a lance. What's on your mind, Diment?"

"You and Stanwick with me. And Pamela. The rest of you get along to the passenger cabins and strap down."

He shoved through the press for the communications trunk and went up the companion three treads at a time.

Two modules up, the control cabin filled the full width of the ship, with circular ports in every quadrant to give a bird's-eye view of the port. In the center, a raised, gymbal-mounted command island was manned by four android figures, waiting for the word. Round the perimeter were six acceleration couches for VIPs traveling on the bridge.

It was what he had hoped for, but had not truly expected to find. It was the jackpot of all breaks. He said, "Talk to them Pamela. Use all that expertise you picked up on the assembly line. Tell them that the state is in danger. Crash countdown. Lift off as of now from this site."

He heard her begin, using the Chief Organizer's voice to leave no persuasive stone unturned.

Meanwhile, he roamed around looking at charts, picking a point on the turning world for a landfall. Finally, he said, "There. That should do it. Not too big and not too small. Far enough into Eastern Hem to make us hard to find. Ishigaki Island. The coastal strip. Kabira Bay. Take the reference, Pamela, and feed it into those tin ears."

She was doing all right. The ship had come alive.

Diment's earlier informant had been right on all counts. The military craft were held at instant readiness in spite of appearances in the pen.

A speaker in the deck head said, "All passengers prepare for liftoff. Do not leave your acceleration couch until the green light glows."

Diment grabbed Pamela Harte and hustled her into a couch, joined her, and passed the holding straps round them both.

As he shot the last clip, XX9 began to move.

The scanner showed them the pad, androids and Organizers scattering from the fireball that filled the packed pen with vermilion flame.

One android had climbed the outer skin looking for the emergency hatch, and his ovoid head appeared briefly in a port. Then he was fighting to grip with one hand and bring a phasor to bear on the glass.

The free arm was being blown back with the bright phasor beam shooting to the sky.

Centimeter by centimeter he pulled it down.

Pamela Harte was saying, "No. No. He can't do it. Not when we've got so far. He *can't*."

As if the psychokinetic force was the last milligram needed to break adhesion, his hand was snatched from the coaming and he fell away in free flight.

XX9 clawed itself into the sky with its silent pilots processing data for a course and a landfall. Green lights glowed in every module. Diment with Williams and Stanwick cut a way into the sealed sector below the cone.

It was all there, with a subsidiary console to arm the warhead. He said, "Bring everybody up, Roy. I want everybody in on this decision."

Tight-packed in the narrow space, faces taut with strain, they listened to his curt exposition.

"There's a chance here to make a change. As soon as we make a landfall, we arm the head and send the rocket back to home on Urania City. By all accounts one is enough. It will disappear from the map. Without the Organizers the cities will have to shift for themselves."

Pamela Harte said, "But will it stop there? It could kill others besides them. Have we the right?"

Williams said slowly, "Do we have the right to pass up this chance? We are the only ones who know the score. Don't think they won't try to find us. They have the means and next time they won't make any mistake."

Diment said, "I'll take a vote. Two-thirds majority says yes."

Hands began to raise. Looking round, he could see that not one watched anybody else for a lead. It was a personal judgment.

He recorded it soberly, without satisfaction, as a fact. "We are all agreed. That is what we will do."

A kilometer distant, a range of dark, forest-covered slopes penned them in. In front the sea was a dark, flat glass, shot with small phosphorescences. There was no moon yet, but starlight was enough to see the broad shelving strip that lay between the hills and the pale band of beach.

A charred shadow marked the site of XX9's landfall and departure. Beyond it was the cairn of stores that had been stripped out of the ship; acceleration couches; the power suit; a miniature radio that was bringing Western Hem newscasts; food; fuel cells; tools; all the metal Stanwick had reckoned could be safely cut away without weakening the structure or altering its handling characteristics.

Pamela Harte had programmed the pilots for a one-way ticket, a bombing trip that would plunge the rocket with its nuclear warhead fully operational, into the center square of Urania City.

Roger Diment and Pamela Harte walked by the water's edge. There was at least another half hour before they could expect to hear of the rocket's return to base. Prodigal with irreplaceable assets, she had kicked off her sophisticated sandals and was putting unfair strain on the soles of her snowflake tights by squirming her toes in the soft abrasive sand.

Diment considered the distant pile of artifacts, arm comfortably round her waist, feeling the supple move of her body under his hand.

It was not much to found a community on. But that might not be the prime weakness. The small human group was an unknown quantity. Williams, Stanwick, and Carol Greer had given some proof that they were tough-minded and reliable. That left seven. There could be a cuckoo in the nest already. Maybe out of any twelve there would be three good, three bad, and six ready to jump either way.

But that was strictly for tomorrow. There was a lot of time ahead to sort the angles.

After the Northern Temperate Zone, the air seemed to fall with a tangible weight, soft and heavy with a scent of ripeness and tropical exotics; with Pamela Harte adding sandalwood as a leitmotif.

Fighting a rearguard for an intellectual approach to the situation they were in, Diment said, "It begins and ends with the human family. Every bid to cut that out of the equation has made a nonsense. Revolutionary France tried it, way back; Communist

Russia; China, before the big bang in the twenty-first; our own dumb generation. They managed it, God help us all, with the help of their own creation. They finally shoved reason out of their heads and externalized it in the Organizers with all their paraphernalia of euphorics and suggestion."

"But it didn't last. There'll be a change now. It may take years, but there'll be a change."

"That's so. You know something?"

"What's that?"

"I don't believe we did it either. We had too much luck. Too much for coincidence."

"We're agents of a special power?"

"Something like that."

"Don't go too solemn on me, Roger."

Pamela Harte broke from his hold and ran ahead into the darkness, her shadowy figure busy in some kind of ritual dance.

But she was laying a paper trail. First, he kicked into her shiny tabard, then her tights laid out like a pointing hand to a family future. Diment stopped thinking about XX9. Whether it hit or not, a man's data acquisition network could only handle one situation at a time. Bent forward like any Sioux tracker on a hot scent, he quickened his step.

It was another illustration that fortune was riding on his back. In a colder country, the trail might have stretched farther.